P61 The liquor had authority

Franchot Tone

A HARD-BOILED CLASSIC

"SOLOMON'S VINEYARD is genuine hard-boiled classic . . . It has *everything*! A private eye; a shoot-out at a roadhouse; necrophilia; a shoot-out in steam bath; mobsters, a crooked police chief; a bizarre religious cult; a knife fight in a whorehouse; kidnapping; a mystery woman with a taste for kinky sex; human sacrifice; crypt-robbing – you name it, detective Karl Craven has to deal with it . . . a brilliant success, and deserves to be ranked with the best of Hammett, Whitfield, Cain and Chandler, et al."

– Art Scott
1001 Midnights

Novels by **JONATHAN LATIMER**
available in Crime Classics® editions

THE LADY IN THE MORGUE

SOLOMON'S VINEYARD

SOLOMON'S VINEYARD

JONATHAN LATIMER

INTERNATIONAL POLYGONICS, LTD.
NEW YORK CITY

EDITOR'S NOTE

This marks the first U.S. publication of SOLOMON'S VINEYARD in a *trade* edition. (*Trade* is used here to refer to an edition generally available at bookstores. In 1982 a 326 copy limited edition was published in California.) We first learned of the novel's existence in an essay by Art Scott included in *1001 Midnights* (Arbor House 1986). We thank Mr. Scott along with Bill Pronzini and Marcia Muller, who put together the aforementioned book, aptly subtitled *The Aficianado's Guide to Mystery and Detective Fiction.*

– B.N. Hare
Editor-in-Chief
Library of Crime Classics

SOLOMON'S VINEYARD

Reprinted by arrangement with Curtis Brown Ltd.

Library of Congress Card Catalog No. 88-82347
ISBN 0-930330-91-9

Printed and manufactured in the United States of America.
First IPL printing November 1988.
10 9 8 7 6 5 4 3 2 1

INTRODUCTION

You are about to read one of the Great Missing Novels in the history of American Mystery Fiction. Nearly a half century after it was written and first published in Britain, Jonathan Latimer's *Solomon's Vineyard* appears in Latimer's own country for the first time uncut, uncensored, and with its original title in place.

This tale of murder, violence, perverse sexuality, and twisted religion in a corrupt Mid-Western town was, it seems, too much for a 1941 America not yet involved in World War II. At least, that's what Crane's publisher must have thought. The book did not appear in any form in the States until 1950, when it appeared in paperback as *The Fifth Grave.* Even then, at the height of the Mickey Spillane craze, it was toned down and softened.

Britain, on the other hand, two years into the blitz, found that *Solomon's Vineyard* delivered enough of a jolt to provide a distraction from the War. Twenty years after its original publication, a British publisher reissued the book, saying that it "made an immediate impact and has become a classic in the field of rough, tough, thrillers."

Immediate impact. A classic. Yet, though the title is listed, the critical essay on Latimer in the exhaustive work *Twentieth Century Crime and Mystery Writers* discusses *Solomon's Vineyard* not at all. And I, a Latimer fan so staunch I check old reruns of *Perry Mason* to see which episodes Latimer wrote, had never heard of the book until Hugh Abramson of the International Polygonics Library of Crime Classics series asked me to do this introduction and sent me a copy.

So here we are, forty-seven years later, facing that most pleasant of paradoxes, an unknown classic. I think *Solomon's Vineyard* now carries a fascination totally apart from the story itself. We'll get to that in a minute. In the meantime, I'll just say that I think it was worth the wait.

Jonathan Latimer was born in Chicago in 1906. He attended Knox College in Galesburg, Illinois, where he was named to Phi Beta Kappa and elected (according to an author bio on one of his books) Most Unpopular Man on Campus. From 1930 to 1933, he was a newspaper reporter.

In 1935, he published *Murder in the Madhouse,* a private eye novel set just where the title says. It was the first of five Bill Crane mysteries.

The Bill Crane novels (the others are *Headed for a Hearse,* 1935; *The Lady in the Morgue,* 1936; *The Dead Don't Care,* 1938; and *Red Gardenias,* 1939) have secured Latimer's place in the history of the private eye novel. Along with Hammett's *The Thin Man,* the Crane books helped create and popularize what has been variously called the "screwball comedy", "nothing sacred", "wacky" or "gin-soaked *cum* sex" school of mystery novel, a tradition carried on through the forties and beyond by Craig Rice and others.

The Crane novels are all very good. Latimer's ear for realistic dialog was second to none. In fact, his reporting may have been *too* good. At least one edition of *Headed for a Hearse* was censored, this time because the cast of 1930's tough guys was careless of the way they tossed around racial and ethnic slurs. The books sold well. Preston Foster played Crane in a couple of movies.

By 1940, Bill Crane was married off and retired.

Latimer had begun the screenwriting that would be his primary occupation for the rest of his career. He was also doing some ghostwriting for Harold Ickes, then Secretary of the Interior. It was in the middle of all this that he wrote *Solomon's Vineyard*.

America entered the War in December, 1941. Latimer spent 1942 to 1945 in the Navy. When the War ended, he returned to Hollywood. He turned out a lot of movies, most notably his adaptation (with Harold Goldman) of Kenneth Fearing's *The Big Clock*, which starred Ray Milland and Charles Laughton. He published just two more novels – *Sinners and Shrouds* (1956) and *Black is the Fashion for Dying* (1959). These were good, solid, 1950's thrillers, enlivened by Latimer's skill with the language. From 1960 to 1965, he was a staff writer for the *Perry Mason* series, turning out some of the best episodes of that remarkably successful show. He died in 1983 at the age of seventy-six.

A concept turns up from time to time in science fiction that there is a place where past, present, and future all exist together. A place where, during your evening constitutional, you are as likely to meet Julius Caesar or your own great-great-grandson as you are to see your next door neighbor.

If we think of the private eye novel as the universe, *Solomon's Vineyard* is that place. As narrator Karl Craven says in the introductory note, "This is a wild one. Maybe the wildest yet. It's got everything but an abortion and a tornado."

It's got echoes of Hammett. Not *The Thin Man*, this time, though plenty of booze is consumed. The Hammett references are to *Red Harvest* and *The Maltese Falcon*.

"Karl Craven" is not our hero's real name; like the Op, his true name is never revealed. Also like the Op, Craven describes himself as fat, though in this case, he is big as well, having played tackle for the University of Iowa.

The name "Craven" is Latimer's little joke – or Craven's. Every once in a while, we get to see the fear behind the toughness. Hardly anybody but a tough-guy PI would call his behavior or attitude craven. Merely sane.

The allusions to the *Falcon* are plot elements. Craven has to solve the murder of his partner, a man he didn't like. He faces temptation, sexual and otherwise, from a fascinating, evil woman.

Every writer is influenced in one way or another by what has gone before. What I wonder about is how a book with such a limited domestic circulation seems to foreshadow so many later developments in the field. The people of the Vineyard could be the midwestern branch of the alien-smuggling cult in Ross Macdonald's first Lew Archer novel, *The Moving Target*. And *Solomon's Vineyard* touches on one of Macdonald's recurring plots – the innocent child or youth who must be rescued even in the face of her own determination to rush toward deadly danger.

But the writer Latimer is most strongly anticipating here is Mickey Spillane. I can't *tell* you how much like a Mike Hammer novel *Solomon's Vineyard* is. Or rather I could, but I would spoil it for you. Let me just say that in style, plot and denouement Spillane had been anticipated.

This is to take nothing away from Spillane, who has been treated less fairly by the critical establishment than practically any writer I can think of. But it is interesting to speculate what would have happened if *Solomon's Vineyard* had received American publication when it was first written. Or if Latimer hadn't written it until after the War, when a battle-hardened population would have been ready to welcome it, the way they welcomed *I, the Jury* and Spillane's other urban nightmares. Latimer might never have written those Perry Mason episodes; he would have been too busy counting his money.

It is, of course, impossible to say. It is all too possible, though, to say too much in an introduction. Enough. Enjoy the paradox. Before you lies a classic you've probably never heard of. Dig in.

William L. DeAndrea
Watertown, Connecticut
January, 1988

Mr. DeAndrea, who has won two Edgars for his own mystery writing, is a long-time fan of Jonathan Latimer's.

Listen. This is a wild one. Maybe the wildest yet. It's got everything but an abortion and a tornado. I ain't saying it's true. Neither of us, brother, is asking you to believe it. You can lug it across to the rental library right now and tell the dame you want your goddam nickel back. We don't care. All HE *done was write it down like I told it, and* I *don't guarantee nothing.*

KARL CRAVEN

CHAPTER 1

From the way her buttocks looked under the black silk dress, I knew she'd be good in bed. The silk was tight and under it the muscles worked slow and easy. I saw weight there, and control, and, brother, those are things I like in a woman. I put down my bags and went after her along the station platform.

She walked towards the waiting-room. She had gold-blonde hair, and curves, and breasts the size of Cuban pine-apples. Every now and then, walking, she'd swing a hip until it looked like it was going out of joint and then she'd throw it back in place with a snap, making the buttocks quiver under this dress that was like black skin. I guess she knew I was following her.

A big limousine waited beyond the magazine stand. I stood in the shadow of an apple machine and watched her get in. Her legs were strong, like a dancer's. I was staring at the white flesh above the silk stocking when the chauffeur closed the door and took her bags from a redcap and put them in front. He gave the redcap four bits and climbed back of the wheel. She had been looking straight ahead, but suddenly she turned to the window and smiled at me. Her smile said: We could have fun together, big boy.

The limousine went away. I watched until it was out of sight. Some doll! Maybe the town wouldn't be so bad after all. It was hot on the platform and I felt sweat ooze under my arms. I showed my bags to the redcap and called a cab. The train began to pull out of the station, the engine throwing steam on a baggage truck. I gave the redcap two bits and got in the cab. It had a sign saying: *Anywhere in town —50c.* The driver didn't bother to close the door.

"Where to?"

"Any aircooled hotels?"

"In this burg?" The driver snorted. "Don't make me laugh."

"What's a good one then?"

"There's the Greenwood." The driver turned around and squinted at me. "Or the Arkady."

"Which is the best?"

"The drummers use the Greenwood."

"Take me to the Arkady."

Hot air rose from the brick pavement on Main Street, making the building look distorted. I saw the town was mostly built of red brick. The pavements and the business buildings and even some of the houses were made of red brick. I saw a cop leaning against the front of a drug store. He had on a dirty shirt and needed a shave. Main Street was littered with papers and trash. A Buick went through a red light by the drug store, but the cop didn't move. There were plenty of cars parked diagonal to the curb, but there weren't many people outdoors. It was too hot.

We went by a movie house, turned left where it said *No Left Turn*, and climbed a hill. I saw a gulley with a shallow stream. The water looked stagnant. In the distance there was another hill with four brick buildings and a smaller white one near the top. There were green fields and grape vines on the hill. The white building looked like a temple. I pointed out the hill to the driver.

"That's Solomon's Vineyard."

"What?"

"You heard of it," the driver said. "A religious colony. Raise grapes . . . and hell."

He looked around to see if I liked the joke. I liked it all right. I laughed.

"About a thousand of 'em up there. All crazy. Believe in a prophet named Solomon." We crossed a square with streetcar tracks and a park. "He's dead. Died five years ago, but the damn fools're still expecting him back."

About five blocks from the square we came to the Arkady. It was a rambling three-story brick building with metal fire-escapes on the front. There were a dozen or so rocking-chairs on the porch. I saw a sign: *Mineral Baths*, and that gave me an idea what kind of a hotel it was. A Negro porter saw us and loafed down the steps.

"How much?" I asked the driver.

"A buck."

"Your sign says anywhere in town for fifty cents."

He shifted a plug of tobacco to the left side of his mouth. "Don't always believe in signs, mister."

He had shifty eyes and his lips were stained yellow from the tobacco. He looked like a ball player I used to know. I got out a fifty-cent piece and flipped it in his face. "Give the porter my bags," I said.

He snarled and I got ready to hit him, and then his face fell apart. He gave the bags to the Negro. There was a red mark where the coin had caught the bridge of his nose. He bent down to pick it off the floorboard and I went up the stairs and across the veranda and into the lobby. The air inside stank of incense. I saw potted palms and heavy mahogany furniture and brass spittoons. Three women were sitting by the reception desk. The clerk was a small man with a smile and coy brown eyes. He had on a red necktie. I wrote Karl Craven on the register.

"Have you a reservation, Mr Craven?" the clerk asked.

I looked at all the keys in the boxes. "What the hell would I need a reservation for?" I asked.

He giggled. He got out a key and gave it to the Negro. "We have to ask," he said. "It impresses *some* people."

I went to the elevator. The women were looking at me. One of them was younger than the others; a pretty redhead with her skirt pulled high over crossed legs. Her face was sullen, and when I looked at her she stared right back at me. She had beautiful legs.

The elevator made it to the third floor and the porter led me to 317. He put the bags down, and while he opened the windows I took a gander at the room. There were twin beds and a big dresser with a white stain where some gin had spilled, and a couple of big chairs. There was a Bible and a phone book on the dresser. There was a patch in one of the green bedspreads. By the door the rug was worn. On a table between the beds was an old-fashioned telephone with an unpainted metal base and a transparent celluloid mouthpiece.

The Negro finished the windows. He looked in the bathroom and the closet. He was stalling for a tip. "Boy, who's the babe in the lobby?" I asked him.

"The young one?"

"The redhead."

"That's Miss Ginger. She's a friend of Mr Pug Banta."

I remembered the name. He was a former East St Louis gangster. Not an important hood, though. He'd run alky and killed a couple of guys in the old days. He was tough enough, but he never was a big shot. I remembered he was supposed to be running a bunch of roadhouses somewhere further west.

"And Mr Banta wouldn't like it if I fooled around?"

"No, sir." The Negro was positive about it. "Sure wouldn't like it."

"Well, I got another chance," I said. "A very swell blonde. She's got a chauffeur."

The Negro said: "That's the Princess."

"The hell!" I said. "What Princess?"

"She live at the Vineyard. Head of the women there."

"The place up on the hill?"

"Yes, sir."

"What's your name?"

"Charles."

"Well, Charles, what are they like up there?"

"Oh, they all very holy."

"I couldn't call up and ask the Princess for a date?"

His eyes got big at the idea. "No, sir," he said. "No, sir."

I threw him a quarter, but he didn't go away.

"I can . . ." he began.

"How young?"

" 'Most any age."

"I like 'em around fourteen."

His eyes spread out. "Mister, that's jail bait in this state."

"Well, I'll let you know," I said.

He started to go. "Hold it," I said. I looked in the phone book for Mrs Edgar Harmon's boarding-house. It was at 738 B Street. The Negro said that was only six blocks away. "Okay," I said.

He left. I took off my coat and the shoulder holster and my shirt. The shoulder holster always chafed me when it was hot. I went in the bathroom and washed my face and chest. I dried myself and put on a clean shirt. My old one was wringing wet. Oke Johnson was living at Mrs Harmon's boarding-house. I decided to walk over there. He'd written he had something. We needed something.

The clerk behind the reception desk simpered at me. He looked like a pixie. I thought, quite a hotel; service for all. I went out. I saw A Street to the left, and a block further along I saw B Street. I was in the three-hundred block. The numbers went up on my right. Seven hundred and thirty-eight was a big, red-brick house with maples growing in front. There was a porch and stairs that needed a coat of grey paint. Oke had picked the place, he wrote me, because he wanted to work quietly. He was a smart Swede; the only smart one I ever saw. I went up the stairs and pushed the doorbell.

A fat woman in a black dress with white lace on it came to the door. There was a mole on her left cheek, just past the corner of her mouth. She had been weeping. "Yes?" she said.

"Mr Johnson, please."

Her puffy eyes came open. "Are you from Mr Jeliff?"

"No."

"Oh, you're from the police. Come in." She went on talking so fast I didn't have time to say anything. "I guess you know I sent for Mr Jeliff. He was Mr Johnson's only friend in town. It was funny, him not being a butcher himself. I never knew what he did, though I will say he had plenty of money."

By this time I was in the house. "I'm not from the police," I said.

"Oh," she said. "Why do you want to see him?"

"I'm a friend. St Louis. Has anything happened to him?"

"Oh!" she said. "Oh!" She hurried up the stairs, moving fast for so big a woman. I began to feel funny. It was one of those things you get sometimes, premonitions, it says in the dictionary, that tell you something is wrong. I didn't try to think what it could be; I just waited until she came downstairs with two men. I saw they were plain-clothes cops.

"This is him," the woman said.

The younger of the cops got behind me so I couldn't run away. The other, a middle-sized man with a pasty face, squinted at me.

"What do you want with Johnson?"

"I'd like to see him."

"Why?"

"I'm a friend."

"Yeah?"

"That's what he said," the fat woman gasped. She was out of breath from the stairs.

"Is he in trouble?" I asked.

The cop laughed. I didn't see what was funny. The woman began to weep. I looked at the cop.

"He's dead," he said, watching me. "He got knocked off this morning." I was half expecting it, but still it gave me a jolt. I'd had a letter from him only two days ago. He wasn't in any trouble then.

"My God!" I said. "Who did it?"

The cop behind me spoke. "Suppose we ask you that." His voice was harsh.

"I didn't." I pretended to be frightened. "I hardly knew him."

"Yeah? Then why are you calling on him?"

"I was just looking him up. I'm from St Louis. I used to know him there. Slightly. Very slightly. I got in this afternoon, and I didn't know anybody else in town."

"How did you know . . .?"

The pasty-faced cop broke in. "Save the questions. We'll take him down to the station. Chief'll want to see him."

"I don't want to go to jail."

"Don't get scared. If your nose is clean, nothing'll happen."

"But my name will be in the papers. I'm a hardware salesman. It'll hurt my business."

"That's your lookout," the young cop said.

We started for the station; but on the sidewalk they decided I'd better look at the body. They wanted an identification. We went back up the stairs and into the house. We passed the fat woman, still weeping, and climbed another flight of stairs. I wondered if Oke had been making love to her. He used to say they were all alike with your eyes closed. His room was on the second floor. It was a large room with a bay window, a double bed with a clean white spread, a hand-carved mahogany dresser, and a couple of mohair chairs. I could see an elm tree out the window.

The body was in the bathroom under a sheet. "I don't want to look at him," I said. "I'll get sick."

"A big guy like you!" the pasty-faced cop said.

I said: "I'm not used to bodies."

The young cop pulled off the sheet."It's time you were."

Oke was lying on his side in front of the toilet. He looked smaller dead, and not so fat. He had on a shirt, pants and black silk socks. The pants' fly was unbuttoned. He had been shot just behind the right ear. There was a brown smear under his head, and blood had darkened his blond hair.

"That's Mr Johnson," I said.

We looked at him. At the right of the toilet was an open window. The bullet had come through there. I could see the back yards of three houses.

"Hell of a time to shoot a man," the young cop said. "Just when he was taking a . . ."

"Never mind," the pasty-faced cop said.

The young cop slid the sheet back over the body. We left the house and got in a green Dodge sedan. The young cop sat in back with me. They didn't talk. The station, like everything else, was built of red bricks. We went right into the chief's office.

He was a fat man with a red face and pale blue eyes, and his name was Piper. He had a cigar in his mouth. His salt-and-pepper suit looked as though he had slept in it. An elk's tooth hung from a gold chain on his vest.

"Who's this?" he said, staring at me.

The pasty-faced cop told him. The chief's eyes went over me, and then they went to the window.

"What's your name?" he asked.

I told him Karl Craven. I pretended to be scared. I told him I knew Mr Johnson, but not intimately. I said Mr Johnson used to bowl and drink beer with our crowd in St Louis. I said he had worked for a collection agency. I didn't know what he was doing in Paulton. He'd come into the bowling alley one day about a month ago and said he was living in Paulton. He didn't say what he was doing. He'd asked me to look him up if I ever got there. That, I said, was what I'd been trying to do.

The chief's pale eyes slid over the two dicks. "Beat it," he said.

They went out. The chief took the cigar out of his mouth and looked at it. The end was chewed. He tossed it in a brass spittoon and got another from his vest. He found one for me, too. I took it, bit off the end and lit it. It was an expensive Havana. We blew smoke at each other for a while.

The chief asked casually: "When'd you leave St Louis?"

I found my railway ticket and gave it to him. "This morning."

He examined the ticket, looking at both sides of it. "Then you couldn't have killed him," he said.

"I wouldn't kill him," I said. "I wanted to drink beer with him."

The chief stared out the window.

I said: "If I'd shot him, would I come around later in the day?"

He sucked at the cigar. "People do funny things."

"Not that funny," I said.

I showed him a card that said I was a representative of the Acme Hardware Company of St Louis. That seemed to satisfy him about me. He told me about the shooting. He said somebody had shot Mr Johnson with a rifle from the outside of the house. The landlady had heard him come in about four-thirty in the morning, and a little later she'd heard something heavy fall in his room. There weren't any other noises so she didn't worry about it. Mr Johnson didn't come down for breakfast, but she thought he was sleeping and didn't call him. When he missed lunch, too, she went up and found his body.

"Anybody hear the shot?" I asked.

"The rifle must have had a silencer," the chief said, beginning to look bored.

I said: "That's damn queer."

"I figure," he said, "that Mr Johnson was playing around with a woman. Maybe a married woman." He took the cigar out of his mouth and tapped ashes into the spittoon. "What else would keep a man up so late?"

I laughed heartily. He went on:

"And I figure the husband, or the brother, followed him home and plugged him from the outside with a rifle while he was undressing."

I said: "Husbands don't usually have rifles with silencers lying around."

"That's so," the chief said. His eyes met mine for a second, then went back to the window. "Where're you staying?"

"At the Arkady."

"If we want you, we'll let you know."

The pasty-faced cop was waiting outside. He pointed out the way to the hotel. "It's only five blocks," he said.

I thanked him and started out. The sun was low, but it was still hot. There was no breeze at all. I thought what lousy cops they were, not even knowing enough to frisk me. I hated cops anyway, especially dumb ones. I wondered what they'd have done if I had told them Oke Johnson was my partner.

CHAPTER 2

WHEN I got into my room I wanted a drink bad. Oke Johnson had been a shock, even though we'd never got on together. You don't have a partner killed every day. I telephoned for the Negro. He came to the door and I told him to get me a quart of bourbon and some magazines.

Film Fun and some of those others with photographs of half-naked babes, and *Black Mask*. I gave him a fin.

The room was like a tent in the sun. I could feel the heat coming right through the window-shades. I got out of my clothes and put my revolver in a bureau drawer. On my way to the shower I caught sight of myself in the mirror on the back of the bathroom door and stopped to look at my belly. The knife wound was healing fine. There would be a scar, but what the hell! What's a scar on the belly? I saw I was getting bigger. Every time I looked at myself naked I saw that. It wasn't all fat; the flesh seemed hard enough, but it still kept coming. I thought I'd probably hit the scales at two hundred and forty. That was twenty pounds too much. I thought, well, maybe the heat will take it off. Or those baths downstairs. I went to the shower and turned on the cold water. I got in. It felt fine.

The Negro knocked while I was in the shower. I put a towel around my middle and let him in. He had a bottle of Old Crow and four magazines. I gave him the sixty cents change.

"Charles, it would be nice now if you got me that blonde from the Vineyard."

He rolled his eyes. "You don't want her, Mister Craven."

"How do you know what I want?"

"They say that blonde's poison."

"Listen, Charles, if blondes were poison, I'd have died thirty years ago."

He bugged out his eyes at me and left. I mixed a drink and went back in the shower. I drank under the water. Then I came out and fixed another drink and lay on the bed and thought about Oke Johnson until I got tired. In a way I was real sorry he was dead, especially as it put me on the spot. But I couldn't go after his murderer. There was that job to do first.

I drank and smoked and looked at the dolls in the movie magazines. Then I looked at the brassière ads. Then I tried to read a story in *Black Mask*. It was about a G-man I'd read about before. He was different from the G-men I'd known. Those had always reminded me of Boy Scouts.

This G-man was wonderful. He had a girl who was always being abducted by the smugglers, spies, kidnappers or racketeers he was after. Then she'd send him a note and he'd come and shoot it out with them. Sometimes he'd have to kill the whole gang to get her loose. It was a fine system. It's a wonder J. Edgar Hoover hadn't picked it up.

I put the story down and thought some more about Oke. I hadn't had any reports from him; only the letter saying he had something. He was one of those guys who liked to be mysterious. He'd wanted to spring it on me all at once, the dumb Swede! I knew he hadn't put any of it down in writing. I was completely in the dark, as the saying goes. And it looked as though I was up against something tough. I had to move carefully. I thought I'd better look around the town before I let anybody know who I was. I might pick up something. And people wouldn't be shooting at me with rifles.

It kept getting darker outside, but it didn't get any cooler. I was all right naked, but where my skin touched the sheet there was sweat. Even the part of my neck on the pillow sweated. About eight-thirty I got in the shower again.

When I came out it was still hot. It was going to be hot all night. I put on a shirt and the pants to my seersucker suit and my shoulder holster. Then I put on the coat. The gun made a bulge under the coat, and I shoved it around until it was almost in my armpit. I went downstairs. The lobby was still filled with palm trees and old furniture, and it still smelled of dust and velvet.

I followed the noise of a radio playing dance music and found a bar. It had been fitted up with red-leather and chromium tables and chairs and it looked strange in the old hotel. A couple of salesmen were drinking at a table and a girl was at the bar. It was the redhead I'd seen in the lobby. I sat down at the other end of the bar. The girl looked at me and then back at her glass. I didn't impress her much.

I ordered a whisky sour. The salesmen were trying to promote the girl. They were making remarks about her, but she didn't give them a tumble. One of them was fresher than the other. He kept saying: "Isn't she lovely?" She *was* a very good number, except for too much paint on her face. Her green dress looked expensive, though, and the colour went well with her red hair. And she had beautiful legs, or did I say that? She was drinking a Tom Collins.

I had a second whisky sour. The fresh salesman went over to the girl.

"Buy you a drink, beautiful?" he asked.

"Scram!" the girl said.

The salesman was tall and thin. He had on a linen suit. He looked cocky. "Beautiful doesn't want a drink," he called to his friend.

"Okay," the friend said. He was a little nervous.

The salesman leaned over the girl. "Come on, beautiful," he said. "It'll make you laugh and play."

The girl paid no attention to him.

"Give the lady a drink," the salesman said to the bartender.

The bartender looked at the girl. She shrugged her shoulders. The bartender made her a Tom Collins. The salesman sat with her while she drank it. He talked to her, but I couldn't hear what he said. She didn't play up. Her face looked sullen.

I crooked a finger at the bartender. "A double one," I told him. I figured I wouldn't mind the heat so much if I got lit. The salesman and the girl began to talk louder. He was trying to get her to go to his table.

"I stay here," she said.

"Aw, come on," he said. "We won't hurt you, beautiful."

"No."

The bartender was angry, but he didn't do anything. The salesman took hold of the girl's arm. "Come on, beautiful," he said.

She jerked her arm away. He began to paw her shoulder. I went over to them. "Leave her alone," I said.

The salesman looked at me over his shoulder. "I'm not hurting her."

"Back to your table," I said.

"Say, mister!" He slid off his stool and faced me. "What business is it of yours what I do?"

"Come on, Charley," the friend called.

"What business is it of yours?" the salesman asked again.

I took hold of his coat lapels and pulled him to me and shook him. I didn't hit him. I didn't want to hurt him. I lifted him off the floor and tossed him back to his table. He made quite a noise when he lit. He struck his head against one of the chromium chairs. His friend sat at the table, staring down at him as though he didn't believe what he saw.

I grinned at the girl and went to my stool. I kept my back towards the two salesmen, but I could see them in the mirror. I hoped they would start something. I've always hated salesmen and cops. The friend helped the salesman to his feet. He was dazed; the fall had knocked his wind out.

"Come on, Charley," the friend said.

The salesman tried to get his breath. He began to brush off his pants.

"We'll get a cop," the friend said.

He helped the salesman to the door. "We'll get a cop," he said again. He did not speak directly to me. He didn't want a fight. He went away with his arm around the salesman.

"You'd better watch out," the bartender said to me.

"Why?"

"They may get the law."

"No, they won't," I said.

"The guy'll be awful sore when he comes to."

"Maybe," I said. "But he won't call any law. He won't take a chance on a mashing rap."

"That's so." The bartender took my glass and began to make another sour. "But the next time don't be so rough." He smiled at me. "You scared 'em so they forgot to pay for their drinks."

I liked the bartender's face. He was young and decent-looking.

"I'll pay for them," I said.

The girl came over to me. It was the first time I'd seen her standing up. It was something to see. She had a million-dollar figure, as they say. She was tall, and it was nice to see good breasts on a tall babe.

"Hello . . ." I said.

Her eyes were blue-green. "Thanks," she said.

"That's all right."

"I could have handled him," she said.

"Sure," I said. "But I thought it would be a good way to pick you up."

She laughed at that. "I'm a popular dame tonight."

The bartender put my drink on the bar. "Have one?" I asked her.

"Why not?" she said.

While we waited for the drink she stared at me. Her eyes weren't bold any more, but thoughtful. She was younger than I'd figured. When she saw I was watching her, she looked away.

"Why'd you want to pick me up?" she asked.

"I'm lonely," I said; "and you got a swell shape."

She took the Tom Collins from the bartender. "Well, my God!" she said. "At least the man's honest." She held up the drink. "Here's how."

She liked her liquor all right. We had three drinks. I saw it was nine o'clock. I said it was time for dinner. I asked her if she knew of a cool place to eat.

"Tony's," she said. "But *you* don't want to take me there."

"Why don't I?"

"You just don't."

"Yes, I do," I said.

The bartender looked as though he didn't care about what was going on. I saw him shake his head at the girl. She didn't pay any attention to him.

"Got a car?" she asked me.

"I'll get one."

"And you don't give a damn what happens?"

"Not with you, beautiful."

"Don't start that beautiful stuff."

"I wouldn't go," the bartender said.

"What can I lose?" I asked.

"Plenty," the bartender said.

"Shut up," the girl said.

I grinned at the bartender. "Well, it's your funeral," he said.

"Sure," the girl said.

The check was $7.10. I paid it and we took a cab to a Drive-It garage on Main Street. On the way she told me her name was Ginger.

"Not Ginger Rogers?" I said.

"Ginger Bolton," she said.

I said my name was Karl. I said she smelled nice. I asked her where she got the perfume and the expensive clothes.

"I get around," she said.

I told her I was a hardware salesman.

"You act tough for a salesman," she said.

"That's because I was in the army."

I got a Chevy sedan at the Drive-It garage. I had a card identifying myself as Peter Jensen, 11 Division Street, Fond du Lac, Wisconsin; but the night manager made me lay down a hundred dollar deposit anyway. When Ginger saw my wallet she looked surprised. I expected her to. I went to a lot of trouble to let her catch sight of the wad of hundred-dollar bills in it.

I let her drive out to Tony's. I wanted to look at the town. It wasn't much to see. The street lights were dim and all I got was an impression of many brick and frame houses kept back by lawns from the street. We passed a hospital and the city pumping plant. Then we were in the country. It was cooler. I looked at Ginger. She was intent on her driving and her face was not so sullen.

"What's a girl do in a town like this?" I asked her.

"What do you think?" she asked.

"You'd get sore if I told you."

"Yeah?" she said. "Well, I'm a singer."

"What kind?"

"With an orchestra."

"Where?"

"At Tony's. He's going to open up next week."

"How much will he pay you?" I asked.

"Wouldn't you like to know," she said.

She had a husky voice and I thought she'd probably sing well.

We went off the cement road on to a gravel road. We passed a small lake and turned into a big parking lot. There were half a dozen cars there. I saw a big farmhouse with a neon sign on it: *Tony's.* We went up wooden stairs to the entrance and came into an old-fashioned bar with a big mirror, two bartenders in shirtsleeves, and pyramids of glasses. One of the bartenders said "Hello, Ginger," and then looked at me. He seemed surprised to see me.

"Where's Pug?" he asked Ginger.

"How do I know?" Ginger said.

The bartender glanced at me. I looked dumb.

We had a drink at the bar. I said I wanted to order dinner and the bartender got a waiter. We ordered steaks and green salad. I ordered a bottle of champagne. That made both Ginger and the bartender look at me. After a while we went out to a veranda overlooking the lake. There was a breeze off the water. The waiter showed us our table.

"This is swell," I said.

"Yeah," Ginger said. "But where's our champagne?"

The waiter brought it in an ice bucket. I had him bring a bottle of cognac, too. I poured some of the cognac in the champagne glasses and the waiter put champagne on top. There is nothing that gives you a rear like champagne laced with good cognac. Try it some time. We drank slowly.

"Who's Pug?" I asked Ginger. I wanted to hear what she would say.

"A friend."

"Anybody to worry me?"

"No."

"I'm glad," I said. "I'm steaming up for you."

"He's a louse," Ginger said.

There were people at three tables. One party was large; three men and five women. At the other tables were couples. The big party was noisy and two of the women were climbing all over a red-faced fat man. I thought he looked familiar, but I couldn't see him very well. The cuddling was strictly fun on the surface but the women were really trying for the fat man. He was giving the party.

"Do you think you could go for me, beautiful?" I asked Ginger.

"Not tonight," she said.

"Tomorrow?"

"Let's dance."

I stuck a nickel in the jive box and we danced. Some of the other people danced, too. I noticed one of the women had got the fat man on the floor. Suddenly I recognized him. It was the chief of police. Piper. He was pretty drunk. Ginger danced away from me.

"Don't be so distant," I said.

"That gun of yours tickles me where I don't like to be tickled," she said.

I pushed the holster further under my arm. She danced closer, putting her head on my shoulder. Her body was firm.

"That's better," I said.

"Don't talk," she said. "Dance."

We danced until the record stopped, and then we went back to the table. I noticed one of the bartenders and the waiter watching us. When they saw me look at them, the bartender ducked into the other room and the waiter came over and poured us more brandy and champagne. Then he got our dinner. The steaks were good; burned a little on top, but red inside. I was having a good time. There were only three things I really liked in the world; food, fighting and . . . women. Oh yes, and maybe liquor. And I was having at least two of them.

"How about another bottle of champagne?" I asked.

"Why spoil good brandy?" Ginger said.

We drank about half the bottle of brandy. The big party at the table near the bar-room door kept getting noisier. The liquor didn't seem to affect Ginger, but she got a little more sociable. She told me she'd worked in the chorus at Harry's New York Bar in Chicago, and then had sung at a Chinese joint on the North Side. She'd also done a little radio singing. Her face wasn't sullen when she was talking about her work. She was really interested in singing.

"Ever think of the movies?" I asked.

"Don't pull that," she said.

"I used to work in Hollywood," I said.

"When do you want me to start taking my clothes off?" she asked.

"The hell with it," I said. "I was just making conversation."

"I'd rather dance."

I said "Okay." I put a dime in the box and we danced again. She danced close to me, her body flat against mine, but I had a feeling there was nothing personal in it. I liked it anyway; her body was so young. When we got back to the table I asked if there was gambling in the place.

"Craps," she said. "In the back."

"Let's try our luck."

"All right."

We went across the bar and then through a big dining-room with a dance floor. There was a raised place for a band. "They open this next week," Ginger said. Back of the floor was a door. We went through that into a room with thick green carpet and green drapes pulled close over the windows. There was a crap table and six slot machines. One of the slot machines was for silver dollars. I hadn't seen one that big since Reno. I put a dollar in it and pulled the crank. A lemon showed. A dark man with a green visor came into the room. He looked at us questioningly. I gave Ginger a twenty-dollar bill.

"Try your luck," I told her.

She was surprised at the bill. "I don't get you," she said.

"No?"

"No," she said. "You talk like a drummer for ladies' hosiery, with your Hollywood stuff. But you don't act it."

"Don't let it worry you, beautiful," I said.

She got a double handful of silver dollars for the bill. Then the dark man gave her some dice. "Let's see," I said. I took the dice and gave them a couple of rolls and then I held them up to the light. They were all right.

"We run a square game," the dark man said.

"Thanks for telling me," I said.

Ginger did all right. She made three points before she crapped out. I won ten bucks on a come bet, but when I tried the dice I threw snake eyes, a ten and a seven in three rolls. I was very cold. As Ginger started to roll again, the chief's party came in and began to play too. The dark man gave them silver dollars. One of the women called him Dave. They all looked curiously at Ginger and me. The two women were still hanging on to the fat chief. He was drunk and his face was bright red and he seemed to have a lot of money. He kept forking it out in twenties to the gals, not caring how much they lost. Once I saw one of them, a dark-haired woman about thirty, slip a twenty between her breasts. She saw me watching her and smiled, and I turned back to Ginger. She'd just lost the dice. The chief was reaching out for them, but I got there first.

"My turn," I said.

He looked at me, but he didn't recognize me. He was too drunk.

CHAPTER 3

THE CRAP game began to grow. Another couple joined it, the man tossing out quarters, and a few minutes later a sour-looking guy in a double-breasted blue suit wandered into the room. He watched for a while and then he began to play, acting as though he was dubious about the game. His face was freshly shaved and powdered, but blue-black stubble showed on his jaws. He looked like a Greek. I figured he worked for the house, but it was all right. Ginger was so hot it didn't matter who was in the game.

She had the dice. When she shook them her body shook, too, and it was exciting to see her press against the table to read the numbers. The table caught her just below the hips. She threw for a long time and finally made her point. She left the money on the table and threw a seven. It was hard to read the numbers because of the smoke in the room. She let all the money ride and threw an eight. She didn't look sullen any more. She smiled at me.

"An eighter from Decatur," she said.

She did it the hard way: four and four. The Greek had bet against her, and he said something angrily. Ginger drew fifty dollars and let a hundred ride. The Greek laid twenty against her. She rolled a seven. She drew a hundred and let a hundred sit. The Greek muttered again and took the dice from her. He pulled some other dice from his pocket and dropped them on the table.

"Let's go," he said.

I took his dice and tossed them through the door to the dining-room. I heard them roll across the dance floor. The Greek's eyes got thin-looking, but he didn't move.

"Some house dice," I said.

The man back of the table took his time. He pushed aside the box where he had found the first dice and got a pair from another box. I took those and threw them away, too.

"From the first box."

He took a pair out of the first box. He looked scared. He glanced at the Greek, but the Greek didn't say anything. I gave the dice a couple of rolls. They were okay. I gave them to Ginger.

The Greek stared at me. "Tough guy, hey?"

"Yeah."

Ginger threw the dice against the backboard. They came up eleven. Then she tossed a seven. She was a tropical heat-wave. Her next point was nine and she had to throw for it. I watched her. Her body went into curves every time she pitched the dice. She got the nine, sucked three hundred dollars, and then lost the dice. I figured she was six or seven hundred ahead. The Greek took the dice. Ginger started to bet with him against the house. There was no sense in that. I shook my head at her, but she went ahead anyway. She bet twenty dollars and lost it. She stopped betting. After a while the dice got around to her again. She had her point, nine, when three men came into the room. She looked up, shaking the dice, and what she saw froze her hand. She stood with the dice in her hand.

"Hello, Ginger," one of the men said.

He was short, but his chest and shoulders were powerful. He had mean blue eyes and he needed a shave. He had the longest arms I ever saw on anything more civilized than an orang-outang. He was a towhead and he had a club foot.

"Didn't expect me, did you, Ginger?"

"No."

Nobody moved around the crap table. I felt glad the chief of police was there until I saw his face. The man turned his eyes on me; then came towards me, walking with a limp. One of his friends had his hand in his pocket. Either his finger or a pistol made a point under the cloth. He looked tough. I thought it was probably a pistol.

"Be careful, Pug," said the man behind the table.

Pug stopped in front of me. His face came about to my neck. He snarled. "You the guy with Ginger?"

"Yes."

"Do you know whose babe she is?"

"No."

"Like hell."

"No."

"Well, she's mine."

"She didn't mention it," I said.

He laughed. It was more like a bark than a laugh. I saw one of his front teeth had been broken. It had turned dark. He came a step closer. I backed away. I didn't want to start a play with three or maybe more toughs against me. I looked at the chief of police. He was still scared. Ginger seemed a little pleased, as though she'd planned it. Maybe she had. Maybe she wanted to make Pug jealous.

"Do you know who I am?" Pug said.

"No," I lied.

"I'm Pug Banta."

"Oh."

He moved nearer me.

"I'm sorry," I said. "I didn't know she was your girl, Pug."

He slapped my face. His arm moved so fast I didn't even

have time to duck. My teeth cut my lip. I could taste the blood.

"You'll know it next time, fatty," Pug said.

Ginger looked frightened now. The Greek spoke to me. "I guess you're not so tough."

"What's he been doing?" Pug asked.

"He thinks the game is wrong," the Greek said.

"If you don't like our games," Pug asked, "why don't you go home?"

I kept saying to myself, don't start anything. I wanted to kill Pug. I never could stand being hit by anybody, not even a woman. I wanted to take him and his pals. I could taste the blood in my mouth.

"I like your games," I said; "with the right dice."

"Wise, eh?" Pug said, and hit me on the cheekbone. It was a good punch. I fell back against one of the slot machines. The metal stand tilted and the machine fell on the floor, shattering the glass front.

"Don't get too tough," I told Pug.

He hit me again. The dark-haired woman with Chief Piper screamed. He hit me on the right temple. He hit hard with both hands. I sat down with my back to the wall. I felt blood run from my mouth. I was a little dizzy. He tried to kick me, but I blocked his foot with my arm. The dark-haired woman ran to him.

"Stop that, Pug," she cried.

He kicked at me again. The woman jerked his arm, trying to pull him away. He got the arm loose and hit her on the nose. The blow sounded like a ripe tomato dropping on a cement floor. She went over on her back. Blood spilled from her nose. Chief Piper, his small eyes frightened, started to protest.

"Keep your damn whores in line," Pug snarled at him.

The chief backed away. The blood had gone from his face, leaving it the colour of a turnip. The Greek was grinning, his tongue running over his lips. Pug kicked at me again; not hard this time. It was a gesture. He turned his head to the two bodyguards.

"Toss him out."

They picked me off the floor. Nobody bothered to do anything about the woman. She was sobbing, her breath coming in gasps, blood streaming down her face. Pug had broken her nose. The bodyguards started me out of the room. I looked at Ginger. She stared at me as though she'd never seen me in her life. In her hand was the money she'd won with my twenty. The bodyguards ran me through the dining-room. I was still a little punch-drunk. They halted on a veranda.

One said: "If we catch you again, fatso, we'll cut off your tail feathers."

"And that ain't all," the other said.

They threw me down the steps. I lit rolling, but gravel cut my hands and face. I got up and walked to the parking place. Nobody bothered me. I got in the car and found a rag and wiped the blood off my face. My jaw hurt when I moved it, but I cursed the Greek and Chief Piper and the bodyguards. Then I cursed Pug. I cursed him longest. I decided I would kill him when I got through the job in Paulton. That made me feel better. I started the engine and drove away. For a long time I could see the neon sign, *Tony's*, through the rear mirror.

CHAPTER 4

It got really hot again in the morning. I kicked the sheet off the bed, but that didn't do any good. It was too hot to sleep. My watch said nine o'clock. I got up and peered at myself in the mirror. My face wasn't so bad. There was a blue mark on one cheekbone, and a swollen lip. I cursed Pug Banta again, but I hadn't forgotten I had my own business first. My own and then Oke Johnson's. Somebody would toast for that. I hoped it was Pug Banta. That would tie everything up nice.

I thought about Oke. He'd been killed by a bullet from a rifle with a silencer. That didn't sound like a crime of passion, as the newspapers say. What I'd told the chief about husbands not keeping rifles with silencers in the closet was right. Somebody smart and cold-blooded killed Oke, and it could only have been because of our case.

I shaved and put on a white linen suit and sent four dirty shirts to the laundry and went down to the air-cooled coffee shop. I ordered the sixty-cent club breakfast, with ham and eggs and corn bread. The waitress gave me the *Paulton Morning Mail*. It didn't have anything about Oke's death that I didn't know. My name was mentioned at the bottom of the story. The name Karl Craven, that is. I was a friend of Oke's, according to the police.

I didn't like the story. It meant somebody might take a shot at me with that silenced rifle. Maybe they'd wait, though, to see how much I knew. I'd worry along.

I drove around the town in the Drive-It sedan for a while. There was a haze over everything and the air was hot and still. I found a cop and asked him how to get to the Vineyard. He told me. I drove past the brick school and followed the car-line. Pretty soon I saw the vineyards. They ran up a range of low hills, broken in spots by flower and vegetable gardens and trees, and disappeared over the crests of the hills a couple of miles away. Green grapes hung from the vines. The road ran between low brick walls, but from the sedan I could see people working in the vegetable gardens. They were mostly women, in bright-coloured clothes that looked like Rumanian or Hungarian peasant costumes. Some of the women had red bandanas on their heads.

I came to a big gate with a metal sign over it: THE VINEYARD. Up to the left I saw the buildings. The gates were open and I drove in. There were two big five-story buildings, two smaller ones, all of them of brick, and a big marble temple. That was where Solomon lay in state. I'd read about it in the *American Weekly*. They had embalmed him like Lenin and had put him in a glass coffin where the people could look at him. They were waiting for the Day of Judgment, when Solomon would jump out and lead his people to heaven in a flaming catafalque. That's what the story said, a flaming catafalque, but I never found out what in hell that was.

I drove past the temple and parked in front of one of the smaller buildings. There were some other cars parked there. I got out of the sedan and started to go into the building. A tall guy in a white blouse and black trousers stopped me. He wore boots over the trousers.

"Only on Sunday are tourists allowed, brother," he said.

"I'm not a tourist," I said.

"What do you want?"

He looked damned unfriendly. His hair had been cropped close, almost shaved, and that made his bushy eyebrows seem queer. His eyes were deep-set and they looked as though they had been mascaraed.

"I want to see Penelope Grayson."

He hadn't been paying much attention to me before, but now his eyes poked at me from under the bushy eyebrows.

"What for, brother?"

"You can ask her, brother, after I get through talking with her."

"Are you a relative?"

"No."

"You can't see her."

"If I can't," I said, "I'll be back with a court order."

His face didn't change.

"And if that doesn't work, I'll get a warrant charging the Vineyard with kidnapping."

He didn't like me. He'd have liked to take a punch at me. He probably couldn't because he was a member of the Vineyard. He went in the building. I looked around. I saw a few more men dressed in the white blouses and black trousers moving between the buildings. The clothes made them look Russian. I didn't see any women.

He came out and crooked a finger at me. We went along a brick walk towards one of the five-story buildings. Behind the buildings, in a hollow, I saw barns and silos. In one field a woman was ploughing behind a pair of grey horses. It was funny to see a woman ploughing. We went up the building's front steps and into a big room filled with old-fashioned furniture. A woman about thirty-five with eyes the colour of maple sugar came into the room. She had a soft white face. She wore a white blouse and a red skirt.

"Daughter Penelope," the man said.

I thought I saw interest in the woman's face, but when she turned to me she had no expression at all.

"Your name?"

"Karl Craven."

"I will ask her."

"I come from her uncle," I said.

I saw the maple-sugar eyes light up again. She went out. I sat down on a couch and lit a cigarette. The man touched my shoulder.

"We do not allow smoking, brother."

I put the cigarette out. I started to throw the butt in a waste-basket, but I thought better of it and stuffed it in my pocket. The man stood looking down at me, his face cold and unfriendly. He made me uncomfortable.

"Hot weather we're having," I said.

He didn't answer, just stared at me. I didn't try any more conversation. I sat there and wondered what I'd do if Daughter Penelope refused to see me. That was a funny way to name anybody, I thought. I wondered if all the women at the Vineyard were called Daughter.

The woman came back, saying over her shoulder: "Here he is, Daughter."

Penelope Grayson was thin and blonde and almost beautiful. She was dressed in white. She should have been beautiful, but she wasn't. There was something strange about her face. It was like the face of a person who is blind. What I mean is she looked at me out of grey eyes that really didn't see me. The woman and the man both watched her.

"I'm Karl Craven," I said. "Your uncle asked me to talk with you."

"It's no use," she said slowly.

The woman went away. The man stayed. I turned to him. "We don't need you."

"I will remain."

"Do you want him to stay, Miss Grayson?"

"Yes, please."

She spoke as though she was in a trance, or doped, or dreaming. She stared back at me steadily enough, but she didn't see me. She wouldn't know me again. Her face was queer, as though it was out of focus. The man looked at me smugly.

"Your uncle wants you to come home," I said.

"I belong here," she said.

"He is very worried about you."

She stood with her dull eyes on me. Her skin was very pale. "You must tell him I am happy here."

She looked anything but happy. I didn't understand it. "He is lonely," I said. "You're his only relative."

"No longer," she said. "I am a Daughter of Solomon. I have abandoned my worldly connexions."

I began to feel spooked. It was like talking to a medium. Her voice came out of her mouth, low and soft, but it didn't really seem to have anything to do with her. It was as if she didn't know what she was saying. I wondered if she could be hypnotized.

"Have you anything for me to tell your uncle?" I asked.

"I have no message."

"Will you see him if he comes here?"

"Please tell him I am happy here."

"Wouldn't you be happy somewhere else?" I asked. "Where your uncle would not worry?"

The man tapped my arm. "Daughter Penelope has talked enough."

"Please," she said; "I must go."

"You are keeping her from her duties," the man said.

She started to leave. I got in front of her. "Wait," I said. "Don't you know you're in danger here?"

"I am happy here."

"She is going now," the man said.

His face was hard. He took her elbow and started to guide her around me. His eyes were as black as ripe olives. I hit his jaw with a right uppercut. He fell on the brown carpet, got up on one elbow. He was dazed, but he wasn't out. I got my revolver and split his head open with the barrel.

That put him flat on the floor. I tucked the revolver in the holster. Penelope Grayson stared at me with her wide, drugged-looking eyes.

"Why did you do that?"

"I want to talk with you alone," I said. "You're in a lot of trouble."

She was hearing and seeing me now. I had broken through whatever was wrapped around her mind. She was still dreamy and unnatural, but a part of her was listening to me.

"I am in no danger," she said.

"I have to talk fast, so listen. I am a private detective. I have a partner, Oke Johnson."

I looked at her eyes, but the name meant nothing to her. I kept it simple, as though I was talking to a child.

"He came to Paulton three weeks ago. At your uncle's request."

"A short, fat man?"

"Yes. He was to persuade you to go away."

"He tried, but I am happy here."

I heard voices outside. Some women were coming towards the house. I grabbed the man by his shoulders and dragged him behind one of the couches. His feet stuck out so I doubled up his legs. There was some blood on the rug, but I put a chair over it. The girl watched me dreamily.

"Yesterday Oke Johnson was murdered," I said. "Somebody shot him. You understand, murdered him. It's in the papers, if you don't believe me. Somebody was afraid of what he was doing in connexion with you."

Feet made a noise on the stairs. The girl's eyes were on me. I stared right back at her. I wanted her to believe. "Do you understand what I've told you?" I asked.

Someone came into the room behind me. The girl said: "Yes, I understand." I looked around.

It was the woman I'd seen at the station. The woman with the curves. She stopped by the door and stared at me. She had on a Russian-looking costume, too, only hers was scarlet, both the blouse and the skirt. And beside the others I'd seen, it looked like a number out of Hattie Carnegie's window. She was beautiful. She was surprised to see me, but she smiled, as though it was a pleasant surprise.

"I will go now," Penelope Grayson said.

She glided out of the room. I said, "Hello" to the Princess.

She smiled again and said "Hello."

I went by her to the door, smelling her perfume. It made me think of black lace underwear. I wanted to stay and talk, but I had to get out before my pal behind the sofa began to moan. The Princess had blue eyes and her breasts pressed against the red silk. I smiled at her and walked down the front steps.

It was still and hot outside, and the sun was high in a clear sky. Sprinklers worked over beds of yellow flowers. I walked not too fast to the Chevy, passing several men in white blouses. The men paid no attention to me. I wondered what would happen to me if they got me before I left the grounds. A bunch of religious nuts like those might do anything. I climbed in the sedan and eased her along the gravel road. By the time I reached the street-car tracks outside the big gate, brother, I had sweated plenty, just thinking about being caught.

CHAPTER 5

I WENT up to my room at the Arkady and took off my clothes. I lay on the bed in a pair of shorts and poured myself a glass of bourbon. I drank the bourbon slowly, letting it coat my throat. I wondered if I'd been wrong in telling the girl about Oke's death. I didn't think so. I had to shock her; start her thinking. It was a thing the people at the Vineyard didn't want her to do. They were trying their best to stop her from it. I didn't know if they were doing it with drugs, or by hypnotism, or in some other way, but they were doing it. It was the way some of those places worked. Her uncle had said she was emotionally unbalanced. Those were the kind they liked to get hold of, especially when there was a pile of money too.

I decided I'd done the right thing, even though it meant I was going to have to play it the hard way. Now I was out in the open. No sulking around like Oke Johnson. I took another drink and telephoned down for the Negro. I was kind of glad to be playing it the way I was.

It all came back to something I'd figured out once about the detective business. There were two ways to go along: underground or on top. I never found out which was best. Underground you had the element of surprise on your side, but it was harder to move around. On top you went everywhere, taking cracks at everybody, and everybody taking cracks at you. You had to be tough to play it that way. Well, I was tough.

When the Negro came, I told him I wanted him to deliver a message for me.

"Yes, sir," he said.

"To that doll, Ginger."

The Negro looked scared.

"Ask her if she'll eat with me tonight. I'll be in the bar at seven."

The Negro got pop-eyed: "Mister," he began.

I gave him five dollars. He shut up and left. I looked in the phone book. There was a Thomas McGee, lawyer, at 980 Main Street. The number was White 2368. The pixie clerk answered the phone and I gave him the number.

"I know that number," he giggled. "McGee, the lawyer."

"Jesus," I said. "I thought it was the morgue."

A woman answered the phone. I told her my name was Karl Craven. I said I'd like to see McGee after lunch.

"I'll see if Mr McGee will be free," she said. Then, after a pause: "Mr McGee will see you at one-thirty, Mr Craven."

That was an hour away. I took a drink of bourbon and put on my green gabardine and went down to the coffee shop. I had the lunch with pork chops and mashed potatoes. I was about through when a young punk with a thin, pale face sat on the stool next to me. He ordered a ham sandwich and a cup of coffee. He glanced at me, but when I looked at him he turned away. I wondered if he was tailing me. I'd see when I went out.

I finished lunch and gave the girl a tip. The punk leaned towards me.

"A lady wants to see you," he said.

"Huh?"

He looked frightened. "This afternoon. She's at 569 Green. Carmel Todd."

"I don't know any Carmel Todd," I said.

He slid off the stool and put a fifty-cent piece on the counter and went out. He didn't look at me. I saw he hadn't eaten his sandwich. What the hell! I thought. I went out to the street, but he was gone. I went back and paid my bill and got a cab and went to McGee's office. It was on the fifth floor of a brick building. A girl sat at a desk in the reception-room. She had moist lips and watery brown eyes. I gave her my name. She simpered at me and went in an inner office.

From the looks of the reception-room I decided McGee wasn't so prosperous. The furniture consisted of three wicker chairs and a wicker table with tattered copies of the *Rotarian* on it. Near the entrance was the girl's table with a telephone and a typewriter. There was one picture on the brown wall: a sailing ship on a very blue ocean. On the floor was a grass rug. I sat in one of the chairs and looked at a *Rotarian* for January. After a while the girl came back and said Mr McGee would see me.

The inner office was dark. Heavy curtains kept out the light. I could just see McGee standing behind his desk. He was a tall man with stooped shoulders, and his eyes were set deep in small triangles of flesh. A shabby black suit made him look like a minister. He shook my hand for a long time.

"Please sit down, Mr Cah——" he said.

"Craven," I said. "Karl Craven."

"Yes. Of course. Craven." He sank down behind the desk and began to make washing motions with his hands. "What can I do for you, Mr Craven?"

"Mr Grayson sent me."

"Ah, Mr Grayson!" His eyes gleamed. "What does he want?"

He knew damn well what Mr Grayson wanted, but he wasn't giving anything away. I liked his being smart. I might need help from him.

"I'm supposed to *persuade*"—I let my mouth hand over the word—"Miss Grayson to leave the Vineyard."

He got a package of cigarettes and some matches out of a desk drawer. He gave me a cigarette. "I don't smoke myself," he said. The cigarette was of the ten-cent-a-package variety. I lit it and threw the match in his waste-basket. I took a deep drag of smoke and blew it out my nose.

"I'm afraid," he said, "Miss Grayson will be difficult to persuade."

"I found that out," I said.

"You've seen her?"

"This morning."

His eyes were narrow. "She told you," he said, "that she was very happy."

I nodded. He laughed. It was a queer laugh, a sort of high-pitched giggle. It wasn't what you'd expect to see come out of a guy who looked like a minister.

"You can see, Mr Craven," he said; "that I've been talking with Miss Grayson, too."

He wasn't giggling any more. If you ever look at a rattlesnake's eyes, you'll see the same triangles. He was thinking. The small eyes were bright with thinking. He watched me for a moment.

"What are you?" he asked suddenly.

"A private investigator."

"What firm?"

"My own." I grinned at him. "You think a respectable firm would handle a job like this?"

He leaned over the table. "You are going to kidnap her, then?"

"I don't like the climate in Leavenworth."

"Quite so." He sank back in the chair and made the washing motions with his hands again. "Quite so. What *do* you propose to do?"

"If I knew," I said, "I wouldn't be here."
"True, Mr Craven," he said, giggling. It was weird hearing him.
"You know how badly Mr Grayson wants her out," I said. "You worked for him."
He nodded. "Unfortunately," he said, "the local court refused to grant an injunction against the Vineyard."
"That's why he sent for me," I said.
"Mr Grayson is a very determined man."
"And a very rich man."
He rubbed his hands together. I felt we understood each other, but to clinch it I said: "Naturally, you'll get paid for the work you do."
"I've already received a small fee."
"Five thousand," I said. "Not so small."
"Just a manner of speaking."
"But," I went on, "not so big compared with what he might pay."
"If we can get her out, Mr Craven."
We discussed it. He let his hair down a little and told me he hated the Vineyard. I didn't know as I blamed him: from the way he talked it sounded like a hell of a place. He said he'd been trying to shut it up for twenty years, but every time he'd had Solomon and the Brothers in court they'd gotten the decision. When he was the district attorney, back in 1929, the charge was bootlegging. He knew the Vineyard was supplying the whole county with spiked wine, but the defence proved it had been spiked after it left the Vineyard. Later he got some of the Brothers indicted on a narcotic violation, but the dope he'd confiscated disappeared from the chief of police's office.
"The closest I ever came," he said, his eyes peeping out angrily from the triangles of flesh, "was on a Mann Act violation."
He'd proven two girls had their railroad fares paid from California by the Vineyard. Privately he had forced the girls to admit they'd been used sexually by the Brothers in their ceremonies. But when the case came to trial, both girls denied all immorality. That was two years ago. Since then

the only thing he'd tried was to get the injunction for Grayson.

"The Vineyard sounds like a fine place to live," I said. "Liquor and dope and immorality."

McGee ignored this. He said: "When Solomon died I thought I might get 'em. I thought he was the brains. But they're still smart."

"How long has Solomon been dead?"

"Five years." McGee's eyes darted from me to the window. "Five years Sunday." The eyes came back to me and then went to the waste-basket. "On Sunday his body will be on view."

"Five years and they still look at him?"

"It's quite a sight, if you don't mind the odour."

I asked some more questions about the Vineyard. The colony had been founded in 1868 by the first Solomon, a carpenter from Ithaca, New York, who had a revelation one Sunday afternoon. He convinced his family and some of the neighbours that God wanted them to go into a new land. They'd finally settled in Paulton, then a village in the range country, and planted grapes they'd brought from New York. From the first the settlement had been called Solomon's Vineyard.

The men lived in one building, McGee said, and the women in another. All the property belonged to the colony. The children were kept in a third building. The Brothers became prosperous, selling vegetables, dairy products and wine. People came from all over the country to join them, giving up their personal wealth to the Vineyard when they took the vows.

"Not a bad racket," I said.

The original Solomon died in 1889 after he had picked a five-year-old boy to succeed him, McGee said. When the boy was sixteen, he became head of the colony. He was called Solomon, too, because he was supposed to have been inhabited by the spirit of old Solomon. Under this Solomon the colony became rich and large. He was the one who'd died five years ago.

"Why haven't they picked a third Solomon?" I asked.

McGee wasn't sure. He thought possibly it was because Solomon had announced he was going to return.

"The Day of Judgment?"

"I think so," McGee said, "but I'm not sure, Mr Craven. It's something they don't talk about."

"Where does the Princess fit in?" I asked.

McGee's eyes leaped from the floor to me. "What do you know about her?"

"She was on my train."

McGee said: "Solomon used to take trips incognito. One time he came back with her. He put her in charge of the women and called her Princess. I don't know where he found her."

"Well, she ain't hay," I said.

We talked for a long time about getting the Grayson girl out, but neither of us had any good ideas. I figured it wasn't much good trying again by the way of the courts, and kidnapping was out. I asked McGee if we couldn't show her the colony was phony. That would make her want to get out, and then everything would be jake.

"Yes," McGee agreed, "but where are we going to find something to show her?"

"What about those two California dolls?"

"Dead."

"The hell they are!"

McGee fondled his hands. "A most singular coincidence, Mr Craven. One died soon after the case collapsed. And a month later the other passed away giving birth to a child in the Vineyard hospital."

"They don't fool out there, do they?" I said.

McGee put his hands palm up on his desk and raised his shoulders in a shrug.

"Isn't there somebody who'll talk?" I asked.

"Give me a day," McGee said. "I'll try to think."

CHAPTER 6

IN THE street sunlight stabbed my eyes. The air felt like it had been blown out of one of those driers they use in barber shops. I got a cab and told the driver to take me to 569 Green Street. Carmel Todd. I wondered what she wanted with me.

It was a big, two-story brick house set among elms on a lot that must have been a half-acre. I went up on the porch and pushed the bell. I could hear chimes in the back of the house. Near the top of the door was a funny eight-sided window with eight panes of different coloured glass. It looked like a picture I once saw of an enlarged snowflake. A cute Negro maid opened the door a crack.

"Carmel Todd."

"Carmel don' feel good today."

"She sent for me."

"Oh." The door came open further. "Then she must feel better."

"Yeah, she must."

The maid stepped back with the door. She had on a black silk uniform with white cuffs and collar. She had dust-coloured skin and rouge on her cheeks.

"You know her room, mister?"

"I forget."

"Upstairs and the last one down the hall to the left."

There were oak stairs at the end of the hall. I peered at the living-room as I went by. I saw an Oriental rug on the floor and a combination radio-phonograph and expensive-looking furniture and some lamps with tassels. I went up the stairs and down a hall and knocked at the last door on the left.

"Who's there?"

"Carmel Todd?" I asked.

"Just a minute."

A blonde in a green kimono opened the door. Her hair

had been peroxided the shade of sawdust and on her face was rouge, lipstick and mascara. "Goodbye, honey," she said over her shoulder.

The blonde smelled as though she'd taken a bath in perfume. I mean she stank. I went into the bedroom. A woman was lying under the sheet on a double bed. She had black hair and black eyes and a bandage over part of her face. There was a bottle of medicine on a table by the bed.

"I wondered if you'd come," she said.

"Yeah?"

"You don't remember me, do you?"

"Not with the bandage."

"I'm the one Pug socked. For trying to help you."

I remembered. The one with the broken nose. The one with Chief Piper. I thought maybe it was a touch. Well, she had something coming. I got out my wallet.

"I don't want any money."

I put the wallet away.

She said: "What are you going to do about last night?"

"What should I do?"

"Kill that son of a bitch."

"And fry?"

"You're too smart to fry."

"Maybe," I said. "But, lady, I've been drawing the line at murder lately."

She lay against the pillow, watching me. Her skin was dead white and it made the black eyes look big. She wasn't young, but she was still good-looking. Her shoulders were round and firm. As far as I could tell she was naked under the sheet. I sat down on a rocking-chair. It creaked under my weight.

"But you want to get him, don't you?" she asked.

"I wouldn't mind."

"Neither would I," she said.

"He's pretty tough for a gal to tackle."

"He knocked out my teeth."

The way she said it, it sounded like a good reason for bumping off a man. Maybe it was, at that. A girl likes to hold on to her teeth.

"How do you figure on getting him?" I asked.

"Look," she said, sitting up in bed and almost forgetting the sheet. "I don't know anything about you, but I like your looks. Will you play ball if I've got a good idea?"

"Go on," I said.

She did. She'd been Pug's girl once, she said, and now she was Chief Piper's. So she was talking from the inside. Pug, she said, came to Paulton from St Louis about four years ago. In a few months he got to be the local Al Capone, not that it was much of a struggle. There was nobody very tough in Paulton. And as Al Capone, she said, he demanded and got a fifty-fifty split with the Vineyard.

"Fifty-fifty split on what?" I asked.

"On everything. Liquor, dope, gambling and women."

"The hell!"

"You don't know the Vineyard's back of vice in the county?"

I shook my head. I wondered why McGee hadn't told me. Maybe it wasn't true. No, I believed Carmel. She was telling the truth.

"Pug's just front man for the Vineyard," she said. "He's got plenty of power, but the Vineyard runs everything."

"Who's the Vineyard's head man?"

"Pug gets his orders from the Princess, but she gets them from somebody above her."

She didn't know who that was. But she did know, she said, that Chief Piper was a Vineyard man. He got a grand a month to let things stay wide open. He was afraid of Pug Banta.

I said: "I got that idea."

The district attorney, Carmel said, was on the payroll too. I said it would be hard to shake Pug loose with a set-up like that. Carmel said she didn't think so.

"None of them like Pug," she said. "My idea's this: if things get very hot the Governor will threaten an investigation. Then the Vineyard will throw Pug to him. Pug'll get a long stretch; the Governor will think he's cleaned up the county, and the Vineyard'll go on operating."

I said that sounded good. Carmel said: "Only how can we turn on the heat?"

"You got some beer?" I said.

She rang a bell and the Negro gal got me four bottles of cold Bud. Carmel didn't want any. Her mouth hurt too much to drink. I poured down a bottle of beer and asked her how much crime paid in the county. The monthly net, as near as she could figure it, was about ten thousand dollars. Banta got about half of this, and the Vineyard the other half. She said she didn't know how much the DA took.

I said we would probably need help. She said she couldn't think of anybody she'd trust.

"What about McGee, the lawyer?"

"That old fossil!" she said. "He hates the Vineyard, all right, but he isn't bright enough to do anything about it."

I decided McGee wouldn't be much help. "Anybody in town who really hates Banta?"

"Is there anybody who doesn't?"

"I mean important. Somebody Banta might like to get, too."

She thought for a while. Then she said: "Gus Papas. He's got the only independent joint in the county. Pug's been trying to drive him out."

"Good," I said.

"What are you going to do?"

"I think I can use Gus."

She smiled a little. She looked pretty nice, lying under that sheet. Seeing a woman in bed always gives me ideas. I drank another bottle of beer and told her I'd better be getting along.

"I'll be up tomorrow," she said.

I stood up. The room's windows were open, but no air came in. I could see the elm trees in the yard, the branches drooping with the heat. The beer made me sweat. "I'll give you a ring," I said.

I took the phone number. "Don't call after ten at night," she said. "Mrs Fleming gets sore."

I said: "By the way, who was the guy you sent after me?"

"Charley? He's my half-brother."

"A hop?"

She looked as if she was going to throw the medicine bottle at me. "Of all the goddam nerve!" Then she relaxed. "He's pale because he's had tb."

I didn't believe that. I said: "Does he know why you wanted to talk with me?"

"No."

"Don't tell him," I said. "Don't tell anybody."

"I won't."

I took another look at the sheet and the shape outlined under it. I wondered if I dared lift the sheet. What would I have if I did? I thought. I said "Goodbye, sweetheart," and went out into the hall. I smelled perfume in the hall and heard women laughing in one of the rooms and went down the stairs.

I walked back to the hotel. I asked the clerk if there were any calls for me, but there weren't. I went to my room and pulled off my clothes that now were wringing wet with sweat and got in the shower with the bottle of bourbon. I drank the bourbon and let the water pour over me. It had been a mistake to walk to the hotel.

I decided Carmel was on the level, not that I would trust a whore. I didn't belong to the school of thinkers who held all whores had hearts of gold and would give their last two bucks to keep some guy from starving. All the whores I ever knew, and, brother, I knew plenty, would get you drunk and jack-roll you if you gave them half a chance. But Carmel hated Pug Banta. No woman likes to be socked by a guy who'd throw her down. That made the difference.

Jesus, I was tired! I sat down on the cement floor of the shower and finished the bourbon. I thought about what I had to do with Gus Papas. I would need Ginger and I wondered if she would be in the bar at seven. I began to have the tight feeling in my stomach I used to get before a football game. I saw plenty of trouble ahead. I wondered if it was worth the five grand I had gotten. Hell, yes, it was.

My buttocks had stopped up the drain and the shower water began to sluice over into the bathroom. I got out and mopped up the water and dried myself. I looked at my watch. It was ten minutes to seven.

The bar-room was empty. I sat on one of the stools and ordered an old-fashioned. The bartender pretended he'd never seen me before. He got a bottle of whisky and started to make the drink. A portable radio was playing swing music from New York. I listened to it: they had a good boogie-woogie piano player. He played variations on the 'Basin Street Blues', making it sound like part of a symphony. I drank my drink and ordered another. I looked at my watch. Quarter past seven. I'd just made up my mind she wasn't coming when I saw her. She had on a black evening gown that showed a lot of that milk-coloured skin redheads usually have. I was glad to see her. She came over to me.

"Are you crazy?"

"About you, baby," I said.

"If Pug sees you with me, he'll bump you."

"That punk!"

"You didn't talk that way last night."

"I didn't want to make a scene."

"A scene!" She put her hand on my arm. "Listen. I like you. That's why I'm telling you to scram."

"I'm not yellow."

"You're nuts."

"Maybe you're yellow."

Her eyes got narrow. She didn't like that. "We're talking about *you*."

"You can't be in very good with Pug," I said; "not if you're so scared of him."

"I'm not scared of anybody."

"All right. Prove it by having dinner with me."

She stared at me, undecided. "Why're you so hot to get killed?"

I let her have it. "I'm nuts about you."

Her mouth came open.

"So help me," I said. "I've got to have you. I don't care if Pug's in the way."

"You've been hitting the opium."

"No."

She thought about this. Thinking made her frown. Now was the time to turn it over.

"Believe that," I said, "and I'll slice it thicker next time."

She blinked her eyes.

"Nothing about you gets me," I said. "I'm just excitement-simple. You probably wear corsets and your breasts are broken down."

"They are like hell."

"And I don't like Pug Banta telling me what I can do," I said.

Ginger slit open the zipper on the side of the black evening gown. "Put your hand in there."

I did, feeling the smooth flesh with my fingers. "Okay," I said. "No corsets."

The bartender pop-eyed us.

"Listen," I said. "I've been trying to make you sore, so you'd go out with me, so I could show Banta." I ate the cherry out of my old-fashioned glass. "I'm going to fix him some way. But since you're scared . . ." I stuck a finger at the bartender. "How much?"

"Seventy cents."

Ginger said: "Wait a minute. How tough are you?"

"Plenty," I said.

She gave me a long look. "If I could believe that. Well, what the hell. Buy me a drink. Then we'll step out."

She had a sidecar. I had another old-fashioned. The bartender frowned at us while we drank.

"Ready?" I asked Ginger.

"I'll get my purse." She went out. I gave the bartender two bucks.

"It's none of my business," he said, "but Pug Banta's a killer."

I got out a fifty-dollar bill and tore it in half. I gave him the smaller half.

"How would you like the whole demi-c?"

"Fine."

"Call Pug Banta," I said. "Tell him I'm taking Ginger to Gus Papas's place."

"Jeeze!" he said. "I wouldn't dare."

"Why not? You'll be doing him a favour. He might even slip you a note or two."

He looked at the 50 on the piece of bill in his hand. He wanted it bad. He picked up the telephone and called a number. He asked for Pug. He said something else, and then he put his hand over the mouthpiece.

"He's out."

"Tell it to whoever's there."

"Who's this?" he asked. "Oh. This is Tom over at the Arkady bar. I thought maybe Pug would be interested in knowing his gal just went out with the guy she was with last night. Yeah, Ginger. I think they're going out to Gus Papas's place."

He hung up. I gave him the other half of the fifty. "Thanks," I said.

We got in the Drive-It sedan. I started the motor. There was still daylight at seven-thirty, and the air was hot.

"Let's go to Gus Papas's."

"It's up to you."

"Which way?"

She told me. In three minutes we were in the country. She sat at the far end of the front seat, facing me, her legs curled under her, her back against the door. Her eyes and lips were sullen.

"I'm dumb," she said.

"Why?"

"I know you're up to something."

"Maybe."

"You're not a G-man, are you?"

"God, no!"

"Are you really going to try to get Pug?"

"Listen." I scowled at her. "Nobody slugs me."

"I like you when you look like that."

We turned left past a schoolhouse and went down a dirt road. Trees met over the road, making it dark. The sky was red from the sunset. There was no wind: it was going to be a hot night. We drove along for a time. It was hard to see the road. The trees made it hard to see. I put on the headlights, but they didn't do much good. I could smell clover in a field by the road. After a time we got to Gus Papas's.

It was a bigger place than Tony's. It was kind of a park, as well as a restaurant. There was a small lake with a dock and a line of rowboats, and a ball field, and a lot of trees with tables and benches under them. At one end of the lake were tourist cabins. We drove by the cabins to the main building. Out in front was a gas pump. The building was a hunting-lodge, the walls made of rough-hewn logs and plaster. I parked the Chevy by two other cars.

Inside the lodge there were Indian rugs on the floor and deer and elk heads on the walls. There were some couches and a big stone fireplace. Ginger led me through a hall to a screened porch at the back where there was a bar and a Greek bartender. He was talking to a small man in a white suit. We ordered a sidecar and an old-fashioned. I asked the bartender if we could get something to eat.

"Sure. We gotta special fish dinner."

"What kind of fish?"

"Black bass. Is very good."

"What do you say, Ginger?"

"It sounds all right."

"Okay. Two bass dinners."

We drank our drinks. Ginger smiled at me over the top of her glass. She didn't look quite so sullen. "Here's to Pug," she said. She tried to drink to him, but her glass was empty. I ordered two more. Then we decided to wash for dinner.

The bartender showed me where the men's room was. While I was there two guys came in. One of them had on a tan gabardine suit. The other was a waiter. He had a broom. The guy in the tan suit was bawling him out for not having swept the washroom. I guess that was what it was. They were speaking Greek. The waiter took the broom and cleaned the floor. The guy in the tan suit and I watched him. The waiter got a dustpan and swept the dirt into it. Then he went out.

The man in the tan suit grinned at me. He had a gold tooth. "Damn Greeks," he said. "Loaf all time."

"Yeah," I said. "Say, you're Gus Papas, aren't you?"
"Tha's right."
I held out my hand. "I'm Karl, in the City Clerk's office."
We shook hands. He pretended to know me. Maybe he actually thought he did. Greeks are like that. They can believe anything they think they ought to believe.
"Anything I can do for you, Karl?" he asked.
"Maybe I can do something for you."
The smile went off his face. His lips sort of puffed out, like red rubber tyres. He thought I was going to try to sell him something.
"You know Pug Banta?" I asked.
His face changed again. He didn't look so soft. He nodded.
"I think he's going to try to break up your place."
"How do you know that?"
"Don't get me wrong. I don't know it. It's only something I overheard at Tony's."
The man in the white suit came into the washroom. He was a little drunk. He went to one of the urinals.
"You come to my office," Papas said.
I followed him. There was a desk littered with papers and two chairs. A window looked out on the lake. "Sit down, please; now what you hear?"
"It wasn't much. Maybe I shouldn't bother you with it."
"Do you think it's a bother to me, to hear how Pug wants to break up my joint? Don't make me laugh."
"Okay. I heard Pug talking to a Greek-looking fellow."
"Nick," Papas said. "He used to work for me."
"I didn't know that," I said. "Anyway, I heard Pug say: 'He's been in my hair long enough.' And this Nick says: 'Why don't you drive him out? He's yellow. Break up his joint and he won't stop running until he hits Athens.'"
"Some kid, that Nick," Papas said.
"And Pug says: 'By God! I'll do it. Tomorrow night. I'll make it look like he started the trouble.' And then Nick says: 'If you need a good fella to take Gus Papas's place, I'm him. I know how the place runs.'"
I looked at Papas to see how he was taking it. He looked

scared and mad. He muttered something in Greek. Then he asked: "Why you tell me this?"

"Pug beat me up once."

"He beat up too many people," Gus said. He pushed a button. A waiter stuck his head in the room. "Tell Frank I want him."

I stood up. "Well, I'll be getting back to my girl."

"Wait a minute. Wait a minute. Why you come out here? Why you get into trouble?"

"I thought I'd like to see the fun."

He nodded. "Hokay. There be plenty fun. How many men Pug bring?"

"I didn't hear any more."

"Hokay. We fix 'em."

I went to the door, then stopped. "He'll invent some excuse to get in. That's what he wants to do: get in and start the trouble."

"He no get in."

I went back to the bar. Ginger was waiting for me. "Where the hell have you been?"

"I took a bath."

"I want another drink."

I looked on the bar. She'd drunk both the old-fashioneds. I ordered four more. When the bartender brought them, I gave her one and kept three. "That'll even us up."

She drank hers and reached for one of mine.

"Not scared, are you?"

"A little."

"He'll never come out here."

"He would if he knew."

"Let's eat," I said.

A waiter had set up a table for us in a corner of the porch. There was celery and olives and jellied soup in cups, and beside the table stood a bottle of champagne in an ice bucket.

"I didn't order that."

"Mr Papas sent it," the waiter said.

Ginger stared at me. "How come?"

"Gus is a friend of a friend of mine."

She didn't believe me, but she didn't ask any questions. She didn't talk much while we ate. She was thinking. I knew what about. She was trying to figure out why I should want to make Pug Banta sore again.

"You're quiet."

"I wish you had a chance of beating Pug."

"Let's don't talk about Pug."

"I wish somebody could beat him."

"I'll beat him for you."

"You haven't a prayer. He'll knock you off."

"Maybe he'll get it first."

"I wish," Ginger said.

I poured champagne in the glasses. Then we had dinner. It was good. We ate black bass and drank champagne. The small man in the white suit was joined by some friends at the bar. There were two other men and a woman. They had a round of drinks, and then they went to a table near ours. They began dinner as we finished with coffee and frozen custard. I wondered if Gus Papas was taking my story seriously. I told Ginger I'd be back in a minute and went to the washroom. I went by way of the front entrance. I saw the door was fastened with heavy chain. By a window near the end of the room, standing under a moose head, was a guy with a rifle. He was watching the road. I walked into the washroom, rinsed off my hands, and went back to the table. The guy in the white suit was in my chair. He'd been talking to Ginger. He got up, holding to the back of the chair to balance himself.

"I know you," he said.

"Yeah?"

"I saw you play for Notre Dame against Army. And later against Southern Cal."

I felt the warm glow of being recognized, and at the same time I knew it was a bad idea. At that, the guy had a good memory. Fifteen years!

"You're wrong," I said. "I never went to college."

He ignored me. "Best tackle I ever saw," he said to Ginger. "Come have a drink at our table. I'll think of the name."

"Smith," I said. "And Mrs Smith."

"Best tackle ever lived. Can't think name. You have drink, Mrs Smith?"

Ginger looked at me. "We'll be glad to join you," I said.

He giggled happily. "I knew you would." He led us over to the other table. "Meet Winnie and Jonesy and Peter Davison," he said. The two men stood up. They were both middle-aged. The woman was a little younger. We sat down. "What have you been drinking?" asked the guy in the white suit.

"Champagne," I said.

That surprised him, but he was game. He ordered a bottle for us. Then he told the waiter to start the radio. "Get dance music," he said. He leaned over Ginger. "How do you feel about dancin'?"

"I can take it or leave it."

"Ha, ha. Very funny." He giggled. "How about a dance with me?"

The music started. Ginger looked at me. "Why not?" I said. "He's buying us champagne, isn't he?"

She didn't like it, but she danced with him. The one they called Jonesy danced with the woman. That left me with Davison. He hitched his chair nearer to me.

"What line you in, Mr Smith?"

I was going to tell him I sold machine-guns when I heard some cars drive up. They come fast and skidded to a stop. "They're in a hurry," I said.

"Drunks, probably," Davison said. "What line did you say, Mr Smith?"

"Gunpowder."

His eyes widened. I heard the sound of voices at the front door. Somebody said: "Open up." Davison said: "That's a rather odd line."

There was an argument at the door. I recognized Gus Papas's voice. He kept repeating: "The place is close. The place is close." His voice was high with excitement. "Like hell it is," a deeper voice said.

"Do you handle dynamite, too?" Davison asked.

"Sure."

Ginger forced the guy in the white suit to dance close to the table. He tried to kiss her neck. I couldn't hear the voices any more. Ginger looked at me angrily, but I shook my head. "Who's your friend?" I asked Davison.

"Don't you know him? Caryle Waterman, of the Waterman Drop Forge?"

"A big shot, eh?"

"His family are worth a couple of million."

Gus Papas came into the room. His face was green. He went behind the bar and turned off the radio. He said: "There's some people outside want to speak to a girl named Ginger."

Ginger got pale, but she didn't say anything. She stood in Waterman's arms. He was holding her like they were still dancing. "There isn't any Ginger here," Davison said.

Gus Papas looked at Ginger. "Pug Banta says there is."

Waterman took his arms from around Ginger. "Gus," he said; "you have known me for a long time. You will believe me when I tell you this girl is named Mrs Smith."

I said to Gus: "He wants an excuse to get in."

"Hokay," Gus said. "I tell him to get the hell out of here."

He started the radio again and went out. Ginger walked around Waterman and came over to me. She was scared. "Sit down," I said. "We've been talking about explosives."

"Very interesting business," Davison said.

Waterman hung over the back of Ginger's chair. He wanted her to dance again. "Come on, dear," he said.

"You probably don't know, Mr Waterman," I said, "but they've found nitro-glycerine to be very effective in putting out oilfield fires. Its effect is like that of a giant blowing out a candle. However, it's very dangerous to use."

"Who gives a damn about oilfields?" Waterman said.

I heard angry voices by the door. I heard someone cursing. Then there was a sound of pounding. Somebody swore again, and a shot was fired. There was a moment of absolute silence; then a volley of shots and a crashing of glass.

"My God!" Davison said.

Gus Papas ran on to the porch. "Get inside," he yelled, waving his arm at us. "They shoot you here."

We hurried inside. Papas herded us into his office. Waterman asked: "What's the matter, Gus?"
"Some people try break in."
"By God, they can't do that. Have you got a gun, Gus?"
"You stay here. You no wanta get shot."
"Sure I do," Waterman said.
There was a new burst of shooting. Papas ran out of the room, closing the door on the run. "If this isn't the damnedest thing!" Davison said.
The woman, Winnie, said: "I want to get out of here."
"So do I," Jonesy said.
There was a silence.
Winnie's voice whined: "I never could stand guns."
"It's quiet," Davison said. "Let's go now."
"I wouldn't," I said.
I tried the door while they thought this over. It wasn't locked. "I'll take a look around," I said.
Nobody said anything. Waterman sat on a table by Ginger. She watched me, trying to figure out what it was all about. She slid off the table and came over to me.
"Why won't they let Pug in?" she whispered.
"Gus is afraid he isn't housebroken," I said, going through the door.
She started to follow me. Waterman caught her arm. "Don't go, dear. Stay with papa."
She looked as though she'd like to bite him, but she stayed. I went to the front room with the rugs and the heads of animals. Two men were kneeling under windows with the glass shot out. One of them was the bartender. Another man was lying on the floor by the fireplace. I walked over to him. He'd been shot through the shoulder. His coat was off and somebody had tied a towel over the wound.
One of the men by the window said: "You'd better duck, mister."
I bent down. "Where are they?"
"Back of the cars, I guess," the bartender said. "I can't see 'em."
"How many?"
"About ten."

The other man took a snap shot at something. I fell flat on the floor. There was a jerky series of shots outside and the rest of the glass went out of the windows.

"Holy Christ!" the bartender said.

They gave us a burst with a machine-gun. Then a voice called: "Gus. Gus Papas."

Papas crawled into the room. He crawled with a pistol in his hand, banging it on the floor each time he put the hand down. I moved so I would be behind him if it went off. "Gus Papas," the voice outside called.

"What you want?"

"Either we come in, or we blast you."

"Go ahead," Gus said. "Blow 'im up."

"Look, Gus," said another voice. "We just want to take a look around. We won't hurt you. Or your joint."

"Why you shoot my windows out?"

"Because you shot at us."

"Sure I shoot. Why you try to break my door down?"

"Let's let 'em have it," said another voice. "You can't reason with a Greek."

"Come on, Gus. Use your head."

"You go 'way," Gus said.

There was a shot out in back. The machine-gun let go in front, bringing down an elk's head over the fireplace. It damned near scared me to death. I had my revolver out before I realized what had happened. There was a lot of shooting out in back. The parley had just been a fake to give Pug's men time to close in on the place. There was another burst in front. The man with the bartender by the windows yelped with pain and dropped his rifle. A splinter of wood had torn a gash in his cheek. He started to run across the room towards Papas's office, but a bullet brought him down. He thrashed around on the floor, bleeding from his cheek. I started to crawl across the room. I wanted to get to the office. I saw Ginger and Waterman standing by the door, and the other behind them.

"Go back," I shouted.

Waterman pushed Ginger back and started for the windows on hands and knees. He went past me. "This isn't your fight," I said.

There was shooting on all sides of the house. The bartender was firing out his window. I could hear another tommy-gun in back. Gunpowder smoke began to fill the room. Waterman kept on crawling. "Don't be a damn fool," I called after him.

Papas had gone I don't know where. Ginger and the others were standing well back in his office. Waterman reached the windows and picked up the rifle the wounded man had dropped. He stood up and began to fire at the parked cars. A man came up right in front of him. He had been hiding under the window. He poked a pistol at Waterman and let him have the load. It was as though somebody had opened up Waterman's stomach with an axe. He bent over and hit his head on the floor. Winnie screamed. I braced myself against the floor with my left elbow and brought the revolver to bear on the man and squeezed the trigger. There was the explosion and the *whunk* of lead hitting bone. Part of the man's face tore away and he slid out of sight. Waterman lay on the floor, bent like a pretzel. There was heavy shooting out in back. I crawled to the door of Papas's office. The two men were trying to quiet Winnie.

"Don't, Winnie; don't," Jonesy was saying.

Ginger stared at me, her face excited. "Scared?" I asked her.

"Get me a gun."

I peered into the trophy room. The bartender was still shooting out his window. I could just see him through the smoke. I saw Waterman and the two wounded men on the floor. The tommy-gun began to work again; the bullets knocking pieces off the fireplace.

"If you think I'm going to let you go out there, you're nuts," I told Ginger.

Winnie had calmed down a little. "Is he dead?" she asked between sobs.

"He's fine," I said.

There was a shout outside and the shooting stopped. The

silence seemed strange. I put my revolver away and found a pack of cigarettes. I lit one for Ginger, and then one for myself. The smoke burned my mouth.

"I guess we beat 'em off," I said.

CHAPTER 7

LIKE HELL we had beat them off. We found that out when Davison went into the trophy room to look at Caryle Waterman. The bartender by the window motioned him to bend down, but he didn't pay any attention. He walked over to the body and just as he looked down at it somebody outside let go at him. I saw the flash and heard the *crack* of the bullet, and when Davison went down I thought he'd been shot, too. But he crawled back to the office like a crab.

"God!" he said when he stood up. "That was close."

Winnie asked: "Caryle?"

"He's dead."

She must have known it, but it was a shock anyway. She began to cry. "We'll all be killed," she sobbed. "All of us."

"Now, there," Jonesy said, patting her back.

Ginger sat on Papas's table and crossed her legs. She had long, slender legs. I wished we were alone. Blood always excites me. "It looks like a stand-off," Ginger said.

"So far," I said.

"What are they trying to do?" Davison asked. "I never heard of anything like this."

I took my eyes off Ginger's legs. "Gangsters," I said.

"But they've gone out of style," Davison said. "They don't have gangsters any more."

"Suppose you go out and tell them that," I said.

Winnie said: "Why don't we call the police?"

That was a good idea. I wondered why I hadn't thought of it. I lifted the phone on Papas's desk. It was dead. I tossed the phone on the floor. The crash made everybody jump. I heard a noise in the trophy room. I looked out the door and saw Gus Papas crawling across the floor. He caught hold of the first wounded man, the one by the fireplace, and dragged him along. He brought the man into the office.

"Oh, boy! this is terrible," Papas said cheerfully.

He started to pick the telephone off the floor. "No use," Ginger said. I looked at the wounded man. He wasn't going to die. The bleeding from his shoulder had stopped.

"We hold them off," Papas said.

"Yeah," I said.

"Got three men in back," Papas said. "And me and the bartender here. They don't get in."

He looked pretty happy. He had proved he was a hell of a fighter. He had driven off Pug Banta.

Winnie was sobbing again and the men were trying to comfort her. I crawled across the trophy room to the bartender by the window. He was peeking out through one of the curtains.

"What are they doing?"

"Get your own window," he snarled.

I crawled to another window. By moving the curtain a little I could see out. There was a fire going in back of the cars. I could see the moving shadows of men by the gasolene pump. They were careful to keep out of range of the cabin. After a while two men with torches left the fire. The flames of the torches rose high. They had been soaked in gasolene. The men moved towards us, keeping behind the cars. I saw the bartender raise his rifle. We waited while the men crawled along, their torches lighting up trees and bushes and the parked cars.

Suddenly two machine-guns began to rake the house. I could feel the curtain twitch from the lead. The men with the torches ran for the cabin. I bent my wrist around the window, keeping my body back, and fired where I thought they ought to be. Papas and the bartender were firing, too. I saw a torch sail through the air and land ten feet short of the front door. The shooting stopped. I peeked through the curtain. The other torch was lying near the cars. Somebody must have hit the guy who had it. Papas leaned out his window and took a shot at something. The machine-gun opened up again.

I lay on the floor, listening to the flying lead. I thought we were lucky. The torches could just as well have hit the cabin. We'd look fine trying to put out a fire while they sprayed us with the tommy-guns. But that was over. We'd got two of Pug's men. He wouldn't want to waste many more. Now he'd probably go away.

I crawled back to the office. Winnie had fainted. She was lying on the table and Ginger was washing her face with a damp cloth. The two men were watching Ginger. The wounded waiter was on his back, looking up at the ceiling.

"What happened?" Davison asked.

I told him. Both the men were scared. "I fought in the war," Jonesy said; "but it wasn't like this."

Winnie began to moan. I went through Papas's desk and found a pint of some Greek liquor. When Winnie came to, I made her drink some, and then I had some myself. It was terrible; it tasted like the stuff that oozes out of pine trees. Resin, I guess.

"I'll take one," Ginger said.

I gave her a drink. She made a face. Winnie sat up and Jonesy put an arm around her. "Have they gone?" she asked.

"Yes," Jonesy said. "It's all right now, dear."

The liquor had authority. I felt it in my stomach. I took another drink. Davison and Jonesy watched me. They didn't want any liquor.

"We'll have to get the police," Davison said.

"You go," I said.

"They've gone, haven't they?"

"You find out," I said. "I'm staying here."

"Me, too," Ginger said.

I gave her a drink, and then had another. I was getting a buzz out of the liquor. I sat on the table beside Ginger. Gus Papas crawled to the door. "Hey," he said to me.

He wanted me to come out. I crawled to a window in the trophy room, following Papas's legs. He held the curtains apart an inch for me.

"What they do?" he asked.

I could just see figures moving near the line of cars. The bonfire had gone down and it was hard to make out anything. I didn't know what they were doing. It looked as though they were carrying buckets of something somewhere. That didn't make any sense. I heard the sound of the gasolene pump working. They were carrying gas.

"Damned if I know," I said.

I heard the sound of a bucket hitting the ground. Then two men lit torches at the fire.

The bartender spoke from his window: "They're goin' to try that again."

"Under cover of the car," I said.

"Is good idea," Gus Papas said.

We got ready to let them have it. I thought we could stop them. They'd have to come out from behind the car to throw the torches, and we could wing 'em. I saw one man get in the driver's seat. It was queer; the men with the torches were ahead of the car, not behind it. I heard the starter, and then the car began to move. It was pointed right for the front door. I heard the motor race.

"What the hell," the bartender said.

Suddenly the car jumped ahead; the driver leaped out; the two men threw their torches at the moving car; it burst into flames, picking up speed as it came at us. The car was soaked in gasolene.

"Jesus!" I said. "And it's my car, too."

It came at us in second gear, moving fast enough to make the flames roar. The fire shot fifty feet in the air, thick and yellow. The car was still picking up speed. I heard the sound of the tommy-guns, but right then I didn't give a damn. I wanted to leave. I got up and ran to Papas's office.

I must have looked wild. They stared at me. "Come on," I yelled at them. "We got to get out."

I grabbed Ginger's hand and we ran for the screened porch. They followed. I never saw Gus Papas or the bartender. Just as we reached the porch the car hit the front door with a crash. There was a burst of flames, a hot wind, and an explosion that knocked us to the floor. I lost Ginger's hand. For a second I lay flat, listening to the crackle of flames. I knew I had to get up, but I couldn't. I made myself get up. I got Ginger to her feet. She was dazed. I didn't look for the others. "Follow me," I told Ginger.

I didn't see a door so I went right through the screen, hitting it doubled up. A whole section of screen came loose. I landed on my hands and knees. Ginger stepped through after me. I got up and we ran for the lake. The whole sky was light with the flames. There was still shooting out in front. I ran into the lake, the water sloshing around my ankles, and got hold of a rowboat. I lifted Ginger in, and got in myself. I put the oars in the locks and rowed away from shore. I couldn't make any speed. It was like rowing in a dream. I rowed like hell and we barely moved. I was scared for the first time. Then I saw what the trouble was. I went by Ginger to the bow, and pulled up the anchor. I rowed into the shadow of some willow trees, and then I rested.

"A nice quiet evening," Ginger said.

We looked at the cabin. The flames were on the roof now, and over one whole side. Against the purple sky I saw a big cloud of black smoke. I didn't hear any shooting. The cabin was a goner; all the fire departments in the world couldn't save it. I couldn't see anyone, not even on the shore. I wondered if Winnie and the others had got out.

It was very still on the lake. The rowboat did not move at all. I could see Ginger's face and hands in the light of the burning cabin. Her hair glowed from the reflected light. She looked beautiful and mysterious.

"What do we do now?" she asked.

I moved to her seat. "I'll show you," I said. I swung her across my knees and kissed her. She fought. She jerked away and slapped my face, and when I held her hands she bit my wrist.

I let her sit up. She pulled down her skirt and straightened her dress.

"You're quite a cave man."

I felt the blood on my wrist. "You have a bad effect on me, baby."

"I think all gals do."
"Not like you, baby."
I went back to the oars. I sucked the blood from my wrist and then I began to row across the lake. I thought it would be a good idea if we got the hell out of the neighbourhood. Maybe we could pick up a ride on the main road. There would be trucks.
"Are you sore?" Ginger asked.
"No."
"Next time, ask."
"It's more fun the other way," I said, rowing.
"The jails are full of guys who think that," Ginger said.
The lake was only about half a mile wide. I beached the boat in the mud and carried Ginger to the shore. We walked across a field to a dirt road and down it to the main highway. In the distance I saw the red glow that was Gus Papas's cabin. We stood on the side of the road to wait for a lift. There were crickets under the trees.
"How'd you mix up with Banta?" I asked.
"I was broke, needed a job."
"I'd call it more than a job."
"Yeah?" Ginger said. "Well, it hasn't been."
"And you don't really like him?"
"What do you think?"
The lights of a car lit up the road. The car was coming very fast from Paulton. I heard the scream of a siren and I pulled Ginger to the side of the road. We watched the car go by from behind a bush. It was doing a good seventy miles an hour. We got back on the cement just as the tail light faded away.
"What's this to you, anyway?" Ginger said. "What do you care about my troubles?"
"I care a lot."
"I know what you care for," Ginger said.
"I care for that, too."
She didn't say anything more. I saw a car coming along the road. It was going towards Paulton. "Here's where we hook a ride," I said. We stood on the cement. The car was coming slowly. I thought it was a truck, or a farmer. The

lights made it hard to see. As it came up I jerked my thumb in the direction of Paulton. The car came to a stop.

"Well, look who's here," said a voice.

It was Pug Banta.

CHAPTER 8

WE SLID along the dark highway at forty miles an hour, heading for Paulton. Like hell heading for Paulton, I thought. Heading for a couple of slugs in the gut. I was between two of Pug's boys in the back seat, both with their rods in my ribs. Ginger was in front with Pug and the driver. There wasn't any conversation. The guy on my left smelled of garlic.

We turned off the highway at the city limits. To the left I saw street lights. Goodbye, street lights! I thought. We drove on asphalt, the tyres humming. Pug lit a cigarette, then held the pack to Ginger.

"Have one, babe?"

"No."

He put the pack away. We turned down a lane that was lined with trees and went to a big frame house. We stopped in front of the house. I could hear frogs croaking.

"Joe."

"Yeah, boss," said the guy on my right.

"Take Ginger inside."

"Okay."

Joe got out. Pug climbed out, too, to let Ginger out.

"Pug."

"Yeah, babe?"

"It isn't his fault."

"I warned him."

"I made him go out. I told him it would be all right."

"It's all right," Pug said.

"Oh, Pug." Ginger's voice was husky.

This was creepy. She was badly worried. It didn't look so good for me. I felt funny in my stomach.

"I wanted to make you jealous," Ginger said.

"That's a good one."

"Really, Pug."

"Take her in, Joe."

The guy with me said: "Sit still, dope."

I heard Ginger crying. She didn't say anything to me. Pug got in the back seat. "Let's go," he said.

"Where?" the driver asked.

"To the cabin," Pug said.

We started off. I saw a light go on in the front of the frame house.

I said: "How about a cigarette?"

"Sure, pal," Pug said.

He gave me a cigarette and lit it for me. We came out of the lane and swung around to the right. The car was moving a little faster than before. I took a drag on the cigarette.

"What the hell's the matter with you, pal?" Pug asked.

"Nothing."

"You must be tired of living," Pug said.

"Why?"

"You heard me last night, didn't you?"

"I didn't think you meant it."

"Get a load of that!" Pug laughed. "Pal says he didn't think I meant it." He put his face near mine, trying to see me. "Didn't you think I meant those punches?"

"Were those punches?"

There was a moment when I could hear the sound of the engine and the rush of air. Then Pug hit me, knocking the cigarette against my face. The ashes burned my lips.

"You're doing better," I said.

"By God!" Pug's voice was amazed. "I don't get you, pal. Don't you know I'm going to knock you off?"

"That's what you think, pal."

"Listen to the guy."

"He thinks he's wise," the man on my left said.

We went along in silence for a while. We were all thinking. I wondered if there was a way I could get out of the jam. I wondered if it would do any good to tell Pug I was a G-man. He wouldn't believe it, and he probably wouldn't care, anyway. I'd have to get a better story than that.

Pug said: "I'm trying to think of the best way of knocking you off."

"The Chinese do it with rats," I said. "They let 'em eat the victim."

"Where am I going to get the rats?"

"Well," I said, "there're three in the car now."

I don't know which one hit me; Pug or the guy with the garlic breath. It was the barrel of a pistol and it cooled me for a couple of minutes. When I came to we had stopped by a small shack. I was alone with the guy on my left.

"On tap again?" he asked, poking his pistol in my side.

"Sure."

"You take it funny for a guy whose got no more'n ten minutes," he said.

My head hurt.

"Listen," he said. "If you're nice you'll go without being hurt much. But if you get Pug much sorer, there's no telling what he'll do first."

"When I need your advice I'll ask for it," I said.

I think he wanted to slug me, but my attitude had him worried. I felt him sitting there in the dark, wanting to slug me, but not quite daring to. The driver and Pug came back. They had a roll of bailing wire and some rocks. They threw the stuff in back with me and got in the car. We began to move across a field. I shook my head to clear it. The movement hurt like hell.

"That stuff's no good," I said, kicking the bailing wire.

"You don't know what it's for," Pug said.

"Oh, don't I? You're going to bind me and the rocks up in it, and then dump us in the lake."

"The guy's bright," the driver said.

"Only when my flesh rots," I said, "it'll tear loose and I'll float to the surface."

"Not the way we do it," Pug said.

"It's not as good as cement."

"I ain't got cement."

"That shows you're a punk," I said.

I got ready for the blow. It didn't come. "Listen," Pug said, "you're laying up a lot of trouble for yourself. You can go easy, or you can go hard. I kind of think it's going to be hard."

"Don't kid yourself. I'm not going at all."

"Jeese," said the guy with the garlic breath, "I think he's crazy."

The car came to a stop. Pug said: "Now we take a nice little walk."

"First I want to talk to you," I said. "Alone."

"Come on," Pug said, opening the door.

"Not until I talk to you."

"Go ahead," Pug said. "I got no secrets."

"You scared to talk to me alone?"

"Go ahead," Pug said. "Talk."

His voice was different. He hadn't had anybody act this way on a ride. Mostly, I guess, they begged for their lives. I had him thinking, at least.

"Before you bump me," I said, "you'd better ask the Princess."

There was a silence. In the east I saw a faint light. In an hour it would be daylight. There was a noise of lapping water.

"Why?" Pug said.

"She's going to be sore."

Pug said: "What makes you think I care?"

"You care."

I could almost hear the other guys listening. I was pretty sure Pug hadn't told them about his arrangement with the Vineyard. A guy like him wouldn't. He'd want to act like he was the big boss.

Pug said: "Where'd you get that idea?"

"Ask the Princess."

Pug was silent.

"Listen," I said. "Send those mugs away." I tried to see his face. "You're going to need all the help you can get after tonight."

The car shook a little as somebody shifted his weight. One

of the seats had a squeaky spring. A current of cool air came off the lake.

"Do you know who you knocked off at Papas's?" I asked.

"I wasn't at Papas's," Pug said. "I can prove I was somewhere else."

"Not if Gus talks."

"He won't."

"Don't be too sure."

"Who was knocked off?" Pug asked.

"Did you ever hear of a guy named Caryle Waterman?"

This hit him. He was silent for a minute. Then he said to the hoods: "You guys scram."

They climbed out of the car and went away. "I figured there was something funny about you," Pug said.

"Look," I said. "The Vineyard will be sore as hell about what you've done tonight. You know how they feel about rough stuff."

"Do I?"

I went right on. "There'll be plenty of heat tomorrow. And you'll need the Vineyard's help. But you won't get it if you knock me off."

"Who says so?"

"The Princess, for one."

"Okay," Pug said. "Maybe I'm in a jam. But why should I believe you?"

I told him some of the things the black-haired girl, Carmel, told me. I told him about the ten thousand a month split, and how the Vineyard ran most of the joints in the county.

"And if that doesn't convince you I'm in, ask the Princess."

"If you're lying," Pug said, "I'm going to chop you up like a hamburger."

"Ask the Princess."

"Okay, pal."

I felt better. That gave me a little time. Maybe I could get away before she came. Maybe something would happen. An earthquake, or a tidal wave. I wasn't particular. Pug called the others.

"We're putting this guy in storage for a while," he said.

We drove back to the shack where they had got the wire and the rocks. The car stopped. "Get out."

I got out. Pug told the others to stay with me. They prodded me towards the shack. Pug got in the driver's seat. "Be back in half an hour."

We went in the shack. One of the toughs lit a lantern. It was the driver. The other one grinned at me. He had crooked teeth.

"You must of talked fast," he said.

"I had to," I said.

He thought that was funny. He laughed. The driver was a dark man with a thin face. Something was wrong with his left eye. He didn't laugh. He watched me, keeping his pistol pointed at my stomach. He looked like an Armenian.

"Sit down."

There were three chairs around a stove. I sat in one of them. The shack looked like a place fishermen and duck hunters used. I saw some rods and some old boxes of twelve-gauge shells on the floor. There was a cot in the corner, and over it was a window with a cracked glass. The toughs pulled their chairs away from me and sat down. They kept their pistols on their laps.

I tried to figure an angle. If I could get one of them alone, I'd have a chance. "Is there any water?" I asked. "I'm thirsty."

"He wants water," the driver said.

"Think of that," said the other.

They didn't move. They weren't going to move. I shifted my legs and found I could reach the driver's chair. If I could hook my foot on the leg and pull the chair out from under him, I could make a play for his gun. That is, if the other guy didn't shoot me. I figured I'd have to take the chance. I was gone if I waited until Pug got back. I edged my foot nearer the chair. The driver cracked my shin with his pistol.

"Don't get funny."

The shin hurt like hell. I rubbed it for a while. "You boys play rough, don't you?"

"Shut up."

I could tell by their faces they would shoot if I made

another move. It was a wonder the one with the garlic breath hadn't let go when his pal cracked me. I sat quietly in the chair. There wasn't a damned thing I could do. My mind went to all the times I'd seen it done in the movies. They did it fine there, and in books. The hero was always knocking hell out of three or four armed men. I even saw one movie where he took on eight at once. Franchot Tone, I think it was. I could lick hell out of eight Franchot Tones, armed or otherwise, but I couldn't do anything about the two toughs. Not without getting shot. I wanted to put off getting shot as long as possible. I closed my eyes. I thought, well, nobody will miss me, anyway.

CHAPTER 9

I HEARD the car coming along the road. It was a few minutes before sunrise and the sky was blue. I could see the sky through the cracked window. There weren't any clouds. I had a funny feeling in my throat. I'd been close to death a lot of times before, but I'd never had so much time to think about it. I wished I'd made the break, shooting or no shooting. I would, anyway. The car came up in front of the shack. I heard the motor stop. I heard a woman's husky voice say: "Is he inside?"

"Yeah," Pug said.

She came into the shack and stared at me, standing with a hand on her hip. The lantern and the cracked window made it light inside. Her hair was the colour of a bamboo fishpole, and she had on rouge and mascara, but underneath the paint her skin was good. She had on black slacks and a scarlet shirt and open sandals. She was beautiful. Pug scowled at me over her shoulder. Brother, I thought, this is the third-act curtain.

"So it's you," she said.

I didn't answer. I didn't know what to say.

She turned to Pug. "What's the idea of beating him up?"

That question was like a kick in the belly. It knocked my wind out; I could hear it rush through my throat. *She was going to play along with me.*

Pug said: "He had it coming."

"You're going to have it coming," she said.

"He never told me he was a friend of yours until the last," Pug said. The driver and the Armenian watched him. "You guys scram," Pug said.

They went out. The Princess said to Pug: "We'll get another guy if you keep knocking off everybody who makes a grab for that redhead."

"Get this," Pug said. "Nobody grabs."

"You get this. Another murder or two from you and they'll clamp down on the county."

Pug looked thoughtful. I wondered if he'd told her about what happened at Papas's. "He's already done 'em," I said.

Pug scowled at me. She said "Yeah?" I told her about Caryle Waterman.

"Did you have to pick the richest guy in town?" she asked Pug.

"How'd I know he was in there?"

"You dope!"

"They won't pin it on me. I got an alibi."

"A lot of good that'll do. The Governor won't care about that. He'll start a grand jury investigation and we'll have to close down. Then who'll pay you your dough on the first of every month? Not us. You'll probably have to take up bank robbing, or kidnapping, and then the G-men will grab you."

She was plenty sore. Pug didn't answer her. He stood scowling at me. He was wishing he'd shot me long ago.

She said to him: "Now beat it."

"All right." He went to the door. "How'll you get back?"

"We'll ride, you damn fool. The walk'll do you good. It's only a couple of miles."

Pug said: "It's three miles."

"All the more good it'll do you. Now beat it."

"No."

She slapped his face. It was a hard blow. His eyes got red with anger. Then he turned. "Okay."

She laughed as he went out. She had liked hitting him. She went to the window. I got up and went to her.

"You shouldn't have done that," I said.

"Why?"

"Now he'll have to kill me."

"I don't get you."

"No guy like Pug is going to stand for another man seeing a woman hit him. The slap was all right, but not my seeing it."

"So what?"

"So he'll try to knock me off as soon as he dares."

"Listen, honey," she said. "You couldn't be in a worse spot than you were half an hour ago."

That was true. I should bellyache about Pug. I looked out the window. The sun had come up. It looked like an orange. Pug and the others were walking across the field. She laughed.

"Those small time punks," she said.

I stared at her. She looked pale in the light. I could see the curves of her shoulders and the rise of her breasts under the scarlet shirt. Her skin was white and soft-looking. She turned and looked at me. "Well . . ."

"Thanks."

"I like big men," she said.

Her voice was raspy, like she had a cold. She came up to me and grabbed my arm. Her fingers hurt the muscles. I could smell her perfume. She came close to me. I thought I knew what she wanted. I tried to kiss her. She jerked away.

"No."

"I'm sorry."

She slapped me. She was strong; my cheek stung. She moved in, swinging both arms. Now she had her fists closed. She hit my arms and my chest. I tried to hold her.

"Hit me!" she said.

It was goddam queer. I held her arms, but she got loose. She struck my chest.

She said: "Hit me."

I hit her easy on the ribs. "That's right! That's right!" She hit me a couple of hard blows. Her eyes were wild. She hit me a hard punch on the neck. I hit her in the belly. I heard the breath go out: *ouf!* It didn't stop her. She kept coming in, punching hard.

I gave her one over the kidneys. She grunted and clinched with me. She bit my arm until the blood came. I slapped her. She put her knee in my groin. It hurt. I lost my balance, grabbed for her, and we both went down. We rolled around on the dirty floor of the shack, both panting. She was hard to hold, and every time she got loose she'd hit or kick or bite me. I got over her, holding her down on the floor. She looked beautiful and wild. She bit my arm again and I slugged her in the ribs. She moaned, and then struggled free. My hand caught in the scarlet shirt. The silk tore to her navel.

"Yes," she said.

I got the idea. I ripped the shirt off her, she fighting all the time and liking it. I ripped at her clothes, not caring how much I hurt her. She squirmed on the dirty floor, panting. There was blood on her mouth. I don't know if it was mine or hers. It tasted sweet. Suddenly she stopped moving.

"Now," she said. "Now, goddam you. Now!"

Later we lay on the floor.

"I don't understand you," I said.

"It's fun, isn't it?"

"Yes."

"Then what do you care?"

We had a time getting the clothes to cover her. I had torn them all to pieces. We didn't have any pins. I found some fish-hooks and fastened the black pants to the shirt. She helped me. Then I put the hooks through the worst tears in the shirt. I backed away to look at her. There was a bad rip over her right shoulder. I fastened it and then I kissed her neck. I would have kissed her mouth, but she wouldn't let me.

"What's the matter?"

"I don't want you to."

"All right."

I backed away again. From a distance you wouldn't have known anything was wrong.

"I should take up dressmaking," I said.

"You should take up wrestling," she said. "I feel as though I'd been through a mangle."

"You asked for it, baby."

"Sure. I love it."

"I love it too."

It was bright outside. The sun was well up in the sky. There was no wind; the lake looked like dark glass. Some reeds grew near the shore. We walked to the car.

"Where are we going?" I asked.

"The Vineyard."

I started the engine and backed around so I would be heading for the road. The tyres bumped over something. I saw it was the pile of bailing wire and the rocks. That gave me a shock. I'd forgotten how close I'd been to the lake. I wondered how many other guys lay under that slick water, bound with wire and held down by rocks. I drove to the road.

"To the right," she said.

She settled down in the front seat, watching me through half-closed eyes. She smiled a little. Suddenly I felt scared of her. I don't know why, but I got a feeling. There was no sense to it. She couldn't do anything to me. But there it was.

I drove along the road, passing a few cars. The electric clock in the car said it was seven o'clock. I saw the Vineyard on the hill to the left, the sunlight strong on the big red buildings. From here I saw how big it was, the vines and the fields stretching out for miles. The dark green vines looked cool.

We came to the big gate of the Vineyard. I started to turn in. "No," she said. "Straight ahead." We went on, to a small lane. She told me to turn up that. A hundred yards up from the road, in a clump of bushes, the lane ended. She got out.

"Come on."

I followed her. We went through the bushes. I saw a path that led to the back of one of the big buildings. She halted.

"This is my entrance."

"Oh."

"Will you be able to find it when you come tonight?"

"Am I coming tonight?"

"What do you think?"

"I guess I am."

"You're not only coming," she said, "but you're going to work for me."

"Hell," I said. "I've got a job."

"How would you feel if I told Pug you *didn't* work for the Vineyard?"

"I'd feel bad."

"Well," she said; "drop around tonight."

CHAPTER 10

I DROVE through town to the Arkady and parked Pug's car. Some tourists were loading a sedan in front of the hotel. I was so tired I could hardly walk. I went down a stairway with a sign over it: *Turkish Bath.* A Finn with a square face was sorting out towels in the office. I told him I wanted to steam out. He opened a locker for me.

"Get me a paper."

"Yes, sir." He started out.

"Hey! Get that Negro, Charles, too."

I undressed and picked up a towel and went in the steam room. The air was full of white steam that smelled of menthol. It made my eyes smart. I put the towel on a bench and sat on it. My body was already wet from the steam. I closed my eyes and took a couple of deep breaths. I felt my muscles begin to go soft.

The Finn reached in the door and tossed me a newspaper. I unrolled it. It was an extra on the fire and shooting at Gus Papas's. The headline read: *Gangster Armies Battle!* The first paragraph said that anarchy reigned in Paul County. I read the story. It said that at least thirty men had engaged in a fierce gun battle at the Joyland Recreation Park, and that at least one had been killed. More, it said, were believed to be in the burned building. The shooting had lasted for nearly fifteen minutes. A search was being made for Gus Papas and the owner of an automobile found mysteriously wrecked by the building. The rest of the story was a description of the scene. Pug Banta's name wasn't mentioned.

If it was anarchy now, I thought, what would it be when they found out one of the bodies was that of Caryle Waterman? Then there would be hell to pay: possibly a state investigation. I put the paper on my knees and inhaled the steam. An investigation was what I wanted. They'd find out the Vineyard's connexion with vice and gambling, and that would get the Grayson girl out. Everything would be jake, only I'd probably be dead.

I wondered about the Princess. Why had she saved me? Was she afraid of what I might do to the Vineyard? Or did she need somebody in bed? My guess was that it was a combination of things. She was bored with herself, and not afraid of me. In fact, the opposite. She said she liked big men. I was a big man. But one thing I knew: if I didn't play along with her, she'd let Pug knock me off, no matter how good I was. That would please Pug.

I closed my eyes. The steam was beginning to relax me. I thought, almost contentedly, of the things I had to do. I had to get rid of Pug Banta. I had to get the Grayson girl out of the Vineyard. And find Oke Johnson's murderer. And there was my date with the Princess. That was plenty.

I looked for the Johnson story in the paper. It had dropped back on an inside page. There wasn't much new. The police were following several promising leads, according to Chief of Police Piper. Near the bottom there was a paragraph saying a Mrs G. A. Kellerman, of 467 Fern Street, had seen an odd prowler about the time Johnson was shot. The story didn't say what was odd about the prowler.

I tossed the paper on the floor and came out of the steam room. Charles was waiting for me.

"I want a change of clothes, Charles. And some whisky and breakfast. Eggs and bacon and a sirloin steak."

"Yes, sir." He started to go away.
"And Charles. You remember Ginger?"
"Yes, Mr Craven."
"She come in yet?"
"About an hour ago, Mr Craven."
"Okay," I said. "Scram."

The Finn was a good rubber. His hands were strong, but he was careful of the sore places. I don't know what he thought of my assortment of bites and bruises. He didn't say anything about them. Charles came back with clothes, whisky and breakfast while I was on the table. I made the Finn stop while I had a drink. Then he rubbed me some more. Newsboys were crying 'Extra' in the street. The Finn made me go in a room with dry heat. It was very hot in there; the sweat ran off me. He came with a hose and turned cold water on me. It made me jump around. I dried myself and put on clean underwear. I poured some whisky in my coffee and drank it. Then I drank the orange juice. I felt fine. I went to work on the steak.

"It sounds so crazy," Mrs Kellerman said, giggling.
"Tell me, anyway," I said. "You don't want Mr Johnson's killer to go unpunished, do you?"
"The poor man," she said.
Mrs Kellerman was a thin woman in a blue dress with worn places on the elbows. She twitched when she talked, as though someone was goosing her with a feather. She'd already told me the story of her life, including the fact that her husband had been dead for five years.
"What time was it you saw this prowler?" I asked.
"Just at daybreak." She shook her head. "The police were so funny about my story. They acted as though they didn't believe me. One of the officers had the effrontery to ask if I might have been dreaming. Dreaming! I get little enough sleep as it is without some policemen . . ."
"Please, Mrs Kellerman; what did you see?"
"It was just an accident I happened to see him at all. But I heard a noise; it's funny how nervous a woman gets in a

house, without a man, I mean." She giggled, twitching her body.

"What kind of a noise?"

"Sort of footsteps, shuffling footsteps. I can tell you it frightened me."

It was like pulling teeth. I wanted it, though. I said: "What did you do?"

"I went to the window." She paused, looking at me to see if I was impressed. "And there he was."

"Who?"

"I don't know. How would I? He looked like a priest."

"Like a priest?"

"He had on black robes, like priests wear. And he carried a staff."

"I never heard of a priest with a staff."

Mrs Kellerman giggled. "Neither did I. And his face didn't look like a priest's. It was so pale and—uh—sinister-looking."

"What did he do?"

"He just shuffled by the house and disappeared."

"In back."

"Yes, in back."

"Would you know him again, Mrs Kellerman?"

She thought. "I don't know. It was so early. It wasn't very light." She giggled suddenly. "And I was so frightened."

I asked some more questions, but that was all I could get out of her. A man in a black robe with a staff had shuffled by her house. I began to see why the police didn't think much of the story. You don't see many guys like that, and if you do, other people see them, too.

"Thank you very much, Mrs Kellerman."

"Won't you have some coffee? And a piece of cake. My husband used to say my cake was wonderful."

"I love cake, Mrs Kellerman; I really do. But I have an appointment."

From there I went around to the Drive-It garage to say that the sedan had been stolen. I told the manager I had parked it in front of the Arkady about eleven the night before and hadn't been able to find it when I came out this morning. He took down the details and said he would report it to the police. He didn't seem worried. I suppose the insurance and my deposit took care of him.

I had to wait a long time in McGee's outer office. He was busy on the telephone. I almost fell asleep in the wicker chair. Finally the girl said: "He will see you now, Mr Craven."

McGee leaned over his desk and shook my hand. His skin felt clammy. "Have you heard the news?" he asked.

"I don't know," I said.

His eyes, in the triangles of flesh, were bright. "Caryle Waterman," he said slowly, "was killed in the gun battle at Joyland."

"Yeah? Who's he?"

"The son of our richest citizen."

I whistled. "That's something!"

"Yes. I've been talking with a representative of the Governor. The Governor's going to blow the town open . . . if he can."

"Why can't he?"

He began to wash his hands. "He'll find it difficult . . . as I have." He smiled and tapped his yellow teeth with a fingernail. I got the feeling he wouldn't be too pleased if the Governor did get somewhere.

"But what about Miss Grayson?" I scowled at him. "What are we going to do?"

"I think it would be better if we did nothing for a time, Mr Craven. It is possible the Vineyard will become involved in the investigation. If it does, and mind you, I'm not saying it will, we will have something to talk to Miss Grayson about."

I thought this over. It didn't seem like a bad idea.

"I may be able to throw a few things to the Governor," he said, smiling again. "A few very interesting things."

"Well, we'll give it a couple of days," I said. "When'll I come to see you again?"

"Would you like to go out to the Vineyard on Sunday? That's the day Solomon's body is on view."

"That would be fine."

"I'll pick you up at your hotel." He made the washing motion with his hands. "Say, about ten o'clock?"

"It's a deal," I said.

I got Ginger's room number from Charles, the Negro. It was on the third floor: 347. I knocked on the door. I waited and knocked again. I heard someone move.

"Who is it?"

"Telegram."

"Stick it under the door."

"I can't, miss. You gotta sign."

She sighed. "Okay. Wait a minute."

She moved around the room and then opened the door. She had on a green dressing-gown.

"My God! Aren't you dead?"

"Not me."

She stared at me, her eyes wide. I could see her pyjama legs under the robe. Her red hair looked good, hanging over her shoulders.

"How about lunch today?"

"How'd you get away?"

"Never mind," I said. "What about lunch, sugar?"

"Listen, big boy, you're lucky to be alive. We both are. Let's leave dynamite alone."

I grinned at her. "I thought you were on my team."

"I know what's healthy."

She slammed the door.

I slept the rest of the day in my room. It was hot, but I didn't mind. I felt a lot better when I woke up around six. I had some whisky and a shower, and then I ate dinner in the coffee shop. I read a paper while I ate. There was even more excitement about Caryle Waterman, and the editor, in a front-page editorial, demanded that his murderer be found. The police were still looking for Papas. I began to wonder if Pug Banta's men had caught up with him. It said three more bodies had been found in the building, but that so far no one had identified them. There was nothing at all in the paper about Oke Johnson.

I had left the keys in Pug Banta's car so he could take it, but it was still sitting in front of the hotel. I figured that was nice of him. I drove around to Carmel's house, but the Negro maid said she wasn't there.

"Where is she?"

"I don't know."

"Somebody inside must know."

"No. Nobody know."

"Like hell they don't," I told her. "They don't run a joint like this that way."

A voice said: "Let me talk to the gentleman, Agnes." A big woman in a purple evening gown came to the door. She had been fat, but had recently got thin. The skin on her face hung in folds. She wore a diamond bracelet.

"Carmel is not here," the woman said.

"Where is she?"

"If she wanted you to know, she would have left word."

"All right," I said. "Will you take a message for her?"

"Certainly not."

"For God's sake, why not?"

"We don't do favours for ill-mannered people."

She shut the door. I thought for a minute about kicking it in, and then I went to the car. To hell with it.

I drove around town until dusk, stopping at the bar once for a whisky, and then I went to the Vineyard. I went past the main gate to the lane and turned in and parked by the bushes at the end. I took the keys out of the car this time. I began to feel ticklish in the pit of my stomach. I didn't know if it was fear or excitement. I guess it was excitement; I kept remembering what the Princess looked like lying naked on the floor of Pug's fishing shack. I went down the path to the women's building. Somewhere people were singing; I could just hear the voices. They were singing a hymn. The path ended by a flight of steps. I looked around for the door on the ground level. After I found it I didn't go in, but walked around the building wondering what would be a good way to get hold of Penelope Grayson in case I ever wanted to. There were doors at the top of the front and back stairs, but the windows were all out of reach. I thought the doors would probably be locked at night. It didn't look so good. I walked around to the lower door and knocked.

The Princess smiled when she saw me. "Come in, honey."

I went in. She led me up two flights of stairs and into a room lit with indirect lights. It was a hell of a room. There was a thick blue carpet over the whole floor, and a silken divan as big as an ordinary double bed. The windows had black silk drapes. There was a fireplace and some tables and big chairs.

"Like it, honey?"

"It's swell."

I looked at her. She had on a crimson robe, something like a hostess gown, I think, with a gold belt and gold bracelets and gold slippers. She looked smaller in the robe, but I could still see the curve of her hips. I felt warm in the pit of my stomach.

"Sit down."

I sat by her on the divan. It was like sitting on feathers. It seemed as though I sank down to my hips. I could smell her perfume; heavy and sweet, like the jasmine they have down in New Orleans.

"Are you going to play?"

"What else can I do?"

"You're smart." She patted my leg with a hand that flashed a square cut diamond as big as a lump of sugar. "But, honey, you'll have to give up trying to take the Grayson girl away."

I wasn't surprised she knew about that. Penelope Grayson would have told her. That was probably another reason why she hadn't let Pug kill me.

"I got to make a pretence," I said. "That's what I was hired for."

"Sure." She rubbed my leg. "But don't go any further."

"All right."

"Be sure," she said. "They want her for the Ceremony of the Bride."

"What's that?"

"Never mind. Only, get this. They aren't people you can cross."

She smiled. She had me, and she knew it. She liked the idea. In a way, I did, too.

"What do I do?"

"Let's have a drink, honey. Then I'll tell you."

She got a decanter and a couple of tall wine glasses. She filled the glasses and we drank. It was brandy. "Not bad," I said.

"We make it."

I could feel it mix with that other burn in my stomach. I moved so her shoulder touched my arm. I began to like the perfume.

She said: "I'm so sick of this joint."

"Why?"

"No freedom. I can't go out. I can't get drunk or gamble or wear swell clothes. . . ."

"They look swell to me."

"Shut up, honey. I'm trying to tell you something. I like to dance. I like good restaurants and night clubs, and movies. Here all I'm supposed to do is think about God. It's getting me down."

"You don't like God?"

"I can take him or leave him."

I laughed.

She said: "I was a kid when Solomon picked me up. Eighteen. I wouldn't join the Vineyard as a regular Daughter so he made me Princess. Soly wasn't so bad." She looked at me. "He was a big man, too."

"You like them big, don't you?"

"The bigger the better." She was smiling now. "Soly let me run certain things, and when he died I just kept running them."

"Where'd he find you?"

"In New York."

"In what chorus?"

She looked mad, and then she laughed.

"Wise guy."

"Sure." I reached across her and got the decanter and

filled both glasses. I was getting a buzz from the brandy. "Why don't you leave the Vineyard?" I asked.

"I'm going to."

She got up and went to a desk. The silk robe clung to her buttocks. She didn't have much on under the robe. She came back with a small leather book.

"Look."

It was a deposit book and in it was a folded bank statement. It was the account of Bethine Gleason. She had a balance of $87,567.46. I blinked at the figures.

"When it says one hundred grand, I scram." She put the book away. She sat down by me and drank her drink. I drank mine, too.

"Now, what do I do?"

"You're to work for me."

"Okay."

Her eyes narrowed. "On the surface you're to take Pug's place—work for the Vineyard. The Elders want to get rid of him."

"What do I do for you?"

"You hand over part of the take."

"To build up that hundred grand?"

"Yes."

"What do I get out of it?"

"Well, for one thing, you don't get knocked off by Pug Banta."

"That's certainly something."

"And a salary."

"How much?"

"A couple of grand a month."

"That sounds good."

She said: "And when I've got my dough, honey, you can come along with me if you want."

I poured the last of the decanter into the glasses. "How do you know I haven't got a wife and five brats?"

"I know."

"Don't give me that mystery stuff."

"You're a private dick," she said. "You live at the Bellair Apartment Hotel in St Louis. Apartment 912. Your office is in the Hawthorne Building. You've been in business three years with a man named Johnson. Before that you were a strike-breaker in Detroit, working for a New York firm. Before that you worked for Burns and before that you were in the army. You've got three thousand dollars in the bank and you went to Notre Dame for two and a half years. You . . ."

"My God!" I said. "It's like hearing your own obituary."

She went for more brandy. I was shaken. It didn't seem possible. Even if they knew about Oke Johnson. They were smart, all right. Too smart. I wondered which one of them had killed Oke.

She came back with the brandy. I poured myself one and put it down. We sat in the divan.

"Did you know Johnson had been killed?" I asked.

"I read it in the paper."

"Have you got any ideas about it?"

She touched my leg. "Come on, honey. Let's don't talk business."

Her robe had fallen open a little. "What'll we talk about?"

"Do we have to talk?"

I put an arm around her and tried to kiss her lips. She wouldn't let me. Anywhere else, but not her lips. It was damn queer. I tried again, and we struggled. She began to pant.

"Hit me," she said. "Hit me!"

CHAPTER 11

When I walked to the lane by the Vineyard road, Pug's car was gone. It meant he was getting tough again. But I was too tired to be scared. I caught the two o'clock inter-urban back to town. The motorman stared at me when I gave him my dime, but he didn't say anything. I took a seat in the back of the car and closed my eyes. I thought, Jesus, I'm tired! What a woman! I wasn't good for anything. I wouldn't be any good for days.

"Far as we go, buddy."

It was the motorman, shaking me awake in the town square. I walked to the Arkady and dragged myself up the front steps. Incense almost strangled me as I walked across the lobby. Nobody was at the reception desk. A paper lay on the counter. There was a long story about the shooting. I read down the first column and found one new thing: Pug Banta had been questioned by the DA, but he had an alibi. It made me laugh. Chief Piper had provided it. He declared Pug had been in jail all night, on a speeding violation. "I arrested him myself," he was quoted as saying.

That was a good one! I could see the chief arresting Pug. The clerk came to the desk. He was a new one.

"Anything for Craven?" I asked.

"Oh, yes." He was a fat man with the bread-dough face of a night worker. "Someone in St Louis has been trying to get you."

I told him to put the call in the phone booth. I lifted the receiver and said "Hello." The operator said: "Here's your party, St Louis."

"This is Grayson."

"Oh, hello, Mr Grayson."

"What are you bastards doing down there?"

"We're making progress."

"Baloney! They told me you and Johnson could deliver, but I've seen no signs of it."

I took a long breath. He sounded as though he was going to fire us. I said: "We'll have her out in three days."

"Is that a promise?"

"Absolutely."

"Well, that's better." He was silent for a couple of seconds. "You need more money?"

"We could use some."

"All right. I'll send a thousand down in the morning."

He hung up. I came out of the booth. I rode up in the elevator with the fat clerk.

"Still hot," he said.

"Yeah."

I went to my room. I was sweating. I wondered how the

hell I was going to get Penelope Grayson out in three days. Or in three years for that matter.

In the morning I lay in bed for a long time. I was still bushed. I sent down for coffee and six raw eggs. I dropped the eggs into a glass of bourbon and drank the mixture. Then I drank the coffee. I felt bad that it was the wrong month for oysters.

I propped myself up in bed with pillows and thought about Oke Johnson. He was a big, dumb Swede who thought he was smart. But I had to get the guy who shot him. It would be swell to have people point me out as the private detective who wasn't bright enough to find his partner's murderer. Oke would have had to revenge me for the same reason. I certainly had a great start; a guy carrying a staff. McGee seemed to be the only one who might fit. McGee! I got out of bed.

The Vineyard didn't look like a place where there could ever be trouble. Women were working in the fields, their costumes bright against the rows of green vegetables. Birds looked for insects on the big lawn. I went to the women's building and climbed the wooden stairs and knocked on the door. A faded woman in a black outfit came out.

"I want Miss Grayson."

"Have you been to the office?"

"Yes. They sent me over here."

She looked dubious, but she went inside. I waited on the steps. Pretty soon Penelope Grayson came out. She was in a white costume. She looked more awake than she had last time. She had a good skin. Her ash-blonde hair hung over her shoulders.

"Oh, it's you."

"I came to see if you'd changed your mind."

"You're just wasting your time."

I said: "This is what your uncle hired me to do."

"Why doesn't he let me alone?"

"He wants to help you."

"I don't want any help." She moved closer to me. "Tell him that. Now please go."

"I want to ask you one thing."

"What?"

"Did you tell anyone I spoke to you about Mr Johnson?"

"No."

I watched her face. Her brown eyes were calm. I was sure she wasn't lying. "Please go," she said. "I must prepare my bridal garments."

"Your bridal garments?"

"I am to be Solomon's bride."

She turned and went in the building. Solomon's bride, I thought, must be what they called them when they were initiated into the Vineyard. I stood on the steps for a minute, thinking, and then I walked to the car-line. I was just where I'd been.

I got off the street-car and went to the house where I'd seen Carmel. It was hot and the walking made me sweat. I wondered if it ever got cloudy in Paulton. The blinds were drawn in the house, and it looked as though everyone was still asleep. I rang the doorbell.

After a long time the fat woman I'd had trouble with opened the door. She had on a pink wrapper. She wasn't friendly. "What do you want?"

"Is Carmel there?"

"You've got nerve, coming around at this time of the morning."

She would have slammed the door, but I stuck my foot in it. "Is she there?"

"Get your foot back or I'll call for help."

"Go ahead."

She kicked my ankle. I put my shoulder to the door and shoved. She went over backwards on the floor.

"You bastard!"

I came inside and closed the door. She had a silk nightgown under the pink wrapper. She yelled: "Jim! Oh, Jim!" She got up and started for the stairs. I grabbed her arm and jerked her into a chair. Her hair hung over her eyes.

"You get out of here," she said furiously. "This is a respectable house. I've got a permit."

"Listen; all I want is a civil answer to my question."

A couple of girls came to the top of the stairs. They were both blondes. The fat dame saw them. "Greta, where's Jim?"

The blondes started down the stairs. At the same time a Negro came in a door at the back of the hall by the stairs. A knife scar split his upper lip. He looked big and mean.

"Throw this bastard out, Jim," the fat woman said.

The Negro came for me, moving light on his feet like a big cat. "We don't want no trouble, white man. Just get out."

"First I get an answer to my question," I said.

The Negro kept coming. "You slob," the woman said to me; "throwing women around."

"Come on, white man," the Negro said.

I let him get close to me. "All right," I said. "I'll go."

"Throw him on his ear, Jim," the woman said.

He reached for my collar and I gave him a knee in the groin. He grunted. I let go a right to the face, putting my shoulder back of it. He started to shuffle away and I followed and gave him the old one-two and he went down. He lay on his back on the hall rug.

"Damn you!" said a woman behind me. "Leave Jim alone." I turned just in time to get hit on the head with a lamp made of a Chinese vase. The porcelain, or whatever it was, shattered over me. The blonde who'd swung it stood there, waiting for me to fall.

"What the hell?" I asked her. "What's the Negro to you?"

She came at me, clawing. I caught one arm, jerked it hard and let it go. She spun into the parlour and crashed against the far wall. From the stairs the other blonde screamed. I looked at the Negro. He was trying to get to his feet, an ugly-looking straight-edged razor in one hand. I waited until he got up; then I jerked the rug. He fell on his side. I kicked the razor out of his hand. Then I kicked him in the face. The blonde on the stairs screamed again. I picked the Negro up by his belt and threw him out one of the hall windows.

He took the shade and the lower pane of glass with him. I ran up the hall and shoved the fat woman away from the telephone. I jerked it off the wire and threw it into a big mirror. "Now, damn you," I said to the woman; "where's Carmel?"

She was so scared she could hardly talk. "She went out . . . last night."

"Where?"

"I don't know."

"Who'd she go with?"

She shook her head stubbornly.

"The hell you don't know," I said. "You don't let your girls go out that way."

I grabbed her arms and shook her. Her false teeth fell out and rolled across the carpet. I stopped shaking.

"Chief Piper," she said.

I gave her one more shake. There were a lot of heads at the top of the stairs, but when I looked up they disappeared. I started into the parlour, but a thin man in shirtsleeves was in the way. I hit him and he went down. In the parlour the blonde who'd slugged me with the lamp began to scream. She thought I was coming for her. I went to the big radio in the corner. I picked it up, tearing out the plug, and tossed it across the room. It shattered against the wall. I kicked over a table with two lamps on it. I tore some of the fabric off a davenport. I threw a chair at a big oil painting over the fireplace. I took a metal stand lamp and bent it up like pretzel. I pulled up the Oriental rug and ripped it down the middle. The fat woman and the blonde watched me with eyes like oysters. I came out into the hall.

"After this be more civil," I told the fat woman.

I went out the door. The Negro was lying in some bushes under the window. I didn't worry about him. A Negro takes a lot of killing. I went back to the hotel, walking on the shady side of the street. I don't know why I did that; habit, I guess; I had already sweat up my clothes.

At the hotel the clerk gave me a number to call. Prospect 2332. I went up to my room and took off my clothes and got in the shower. I had a good bump on my head where the lamp had hit me. After a while I dried myself and called the number. The Princess answered, her voice as smooth as cream. "Hello, honey."

"Hello," I said.

"How are you feeling?"

"All right."

"You're coming out tonight, aren't you?"

"I don't know."

"Oh, but I'm expecting you. Don't eat; we'll have dinner together."

I didn't say anything.

"How does it sound, honey?"

"It sounds wonderful."

"About seven."

"All right."

"Goodbye, honey."

"Goodbye."

She hung up and I jiggled the hook on the telephone. When the clerk answered, I ordered a bottle of brandy and a dozen raw eggs.

CHAPTER 12

McGee's old touring car had once been green. It had also been painted black, but this had worn thin and you could see the original green coming through on the hood. The fenders were still black. The speedometer said 53,562 miles, but the motor was smooth. McGee drove as though he had a horse in front, saying 'Giddap' when he wanted to start and 'Whoa' when he was stopping. I was scared he would forget the horse wasn't there sometime and try to stop by pulling back on the steering-wheel. He didn't, though. We got through town without a bump. On the highway McGee opened her up to twenty-five.

"What have you been doing?" he asked.

"Nothing."

"You look a mite pale."

"It's the heat," I said, trying to hide a yawn.

"I don't recall a hotter spell," McGee agreed.

He began to talk about the heat; remembering every wave for thirty summers. His voice made me sleepy. I tried to keep my eyes on the Vineyard's buildings on the hill ahead, watching the sunlight come off the red bricks.

I'd said goodbye to the Princess up there not more than two hours ago. And we had another date tonight, if I lived that long. I yawned. I thought, maybe I could really slug her when she asked to be hit. Maybe that would slow her up.

"Quite a place," McGee said.

"Huh?"

"The Vineyard."

"Oh. Yeah, it is."

"Almost like a medieval colony."

"Sure," I said.

"Only it changed," McGee sighed; "when old Solomon died."

The road was beginning to climb. All around were the green rows of vines. I felt the sun through the fabric top. I thought it would be fun to lie under one of the vines. It looked cool there.

"Old Solomon would never have let you and me on the grounds," McGee was saying. "He ran the place like a kingdom."

"Who runs it now?"

"The Elders."

"I heard the Princess——" I began.

"Whoa, now." McGee pushed down the brake and turned into the Vineyard's driveway. I saw a lot of cars parked by the buildings. "I guess she takes a hand, too," McGee said.

We parked and got out of the car and walked to the mausoleum. There was a line of people on the stone steps, waiting to get inside. They looked to me like townspeople and farmers. Their faces were solemn and they didn't talk much. A lot of them carried flowers. We got in line.

"This temple cost a hundred and fifty thousand," McGee said. "Solomon built it before he died."

"It's bigger than Grant's tomb," I said.

The line moved up the steps. I stared at the building. It was built of marble, the stone kind of pink in the sunlight. Inscribed over the door was: *Vanity, Vanity! All is Vanity.* That was from the Bible, I thought. From the steps I could not see through the door. It was too dark inside.

McGee read the inscription aloud. "Don't look like Solomon took that to mean him," he added.

A woman in front glanced back over her shoulder. She didn't like what McGee was saying. She was dressed in black. McGee didn't pay any attention to her.

"Funny thing," McGee said. "Solomon died the day after the temple was finished. Seemed like he couldn't wait to try it out."

The woman snorted. We moved up the steps. There were people behind us now. I figured at least a thousand people were on the grounds. I saw a brown carpet leading inside from the doorway. The people were walking on that, moving slowly into the darkness. As we came to the door, the line got more compact. My face almost touched the back of McGee's neck, and the man behind was pushing me.

McGee said: "The temple that bootleg built."

We moved into the doorway. The people all around were very quiet. I began to walk on the carpet. I saw candles burning in the far end of the room. I smelled incense.

"The Prohibition Prophet," McGee said loudly.

The woman turned around. "Keep quiet," she said to McGee. "This is a house of God."

"Madam, I am sorry if I have wounded you," McGee said. "But I have a right to my opinion."

"Have you no respect for the dead?"

"For certain dead, yes," McGee said.

The man behind me said "Shut up." Other people were muttering. I heard someone say: "Throw him out." We moved slowly along the carpet.

My eyes had got used to the gloom. There was nothing in the big room except a coffin at the far end and an altar. There were candles on both the coffin and the altar. On the foot of the coffin were heaped all kinds of wreaths and flowers. While I watched a woman dropped a bunch of roses on the pile and went on.

"Do you notice the stink?" McGee asked.

I didn't answer. I was afraid McGee was going to get us in trouble. We went on a few more steps and then I got the stink. It was something! It was like the stink of a horse that's been dead two weeks. It made my nostrils close up. It killed the smell of the incense. I said "Whew!" and got a few dirty looks myself. McGee laughed.

Now we were quite close to the coffin. It was set on a gold and marble table that was about three feet above the floor. The coffin was made of bronze and had leaves engraved all over it. It had a glass top. The table was bigger than the coffin and some of the flowers had fallen on it from the foot of the coffin. About ten dozen candles put a queer light over everything. I heard the woman in front begin to pant. She was looking down through the glass.

"Keep moving, please."

I jumped, almost knocking over the man behind me. An Elder in a white robe was standing across from the coffin. He said again: "Keep moving, folks." He had a deep voice. I tried to see him, but his face was in a shadow. I began to feel spooked.

McGee had reached the head of the coffin. He looked inside, bending down until his nose was close to the glass, and then straightened up, nodding as though everything was all right. I don't know what he'd thought he might see. He walked on, and I was next. I held my breath and peered into the coffin.

Solomon lay on red velvet, face up, blue-grey eyes staring up at me. The open eyes gave me a start. He had on a black robe and on one of his fingers was the biggest diamond I'd ever seen. He didn't look dead at all, except that his face was the colour of wax. The skin made a contrast with his inky black hair. He was a tall man, about six foot six, and he was thin. His face had hollows under the eyes and in the cheeks. He looked nasty and cruel. I could see one tooth back of the blue-white lips.

"Keep moving, please," said the Elder.

I followed McGee out a side door. The sunlight hurt my eyes. I kept smelling the queer odour of incense and flowers and decay around the coffin. It was good to breathe in the fresh air again.

"Well," McGee asked; "what'd you think of it?"

"It's something I won't forget quick."

We went down the stairs. "Take a look around?" McGee asked.

"Sure."

We walked towards the largest of the brick buildings. McGee said that was the administration building. He pointed out the women's building.

"That's where I saw the Grayson girl," I said.

Another of the buildings, McGee said, was for men. The last one was the nursery. It was only two stories high, but it was big.

"Where do the children come from?" I asked.

He led me towards the nursery. "Some of the women bring 'em," he said. "And some have 'em while they're here."

"I thought this was a religious colony. How do they arrange it?"

There were people walking around the grounds. McGee waited until a man and two women had passed by us.

"Have you ever heard of the Walpurgis Night?"

"No," I said.

"Well, that was a night when all the men and women went out into the woods. They stayed all night, drinking and making love and dancing. It didn't matter who you stayed with, it was all part of the ceremony."

"And they have those here?"

He nodded. "Twice a year. One of them is the Ceremony of the Bride. Another is the Wine Festival. That, I have been told, is the wildest."

"Why don't they stop them? Don't they have to register the babies?"

"That's where they're smart. After a woman is initiated into the order, they make her marry one of the men. Then any babies are legitimate, though often the woman never even sees her husband."

"Well, my God!" I said.

I wondered how much McGee really knew. I couldn't tell. He talked as though he knew all about the Vineyard. Maybe he did.

I said: "What is this Ceremony of the Bride?"

McGee looked at me. "You've heard of it?"

"The Grayson gal is to be the bride."

McGee's lantern jaw came open. "Who told you?"

"She did."

"That's terrible!"

I began to get alarmed. "Why?"

He shook his head mournfully. He went over to a bench and sat down. He looked sick.

"What happens to the bride? What's the ceremony?"

"There is a festival one night. And the next night she spends in Solomon's mausoleum."

"The hell!"

"She's supposed to be Solomon's bride."

"And then what?"

"She holds a special place in the Vineyard. She doesn't have to work any more."

"How many Brides are there?"

McGee looked queer. "None."

"None! Haven't they ever done it before?"

"Yes. Every year since Solomon died."

"What happened to 'em?"

"They died."

"Right there in the mausoleum?"

"I don't know. At least their deaths weren't reported until much later."

That was swell! I would look fine if the Grayson girl died.

I asked: "When is this ceremony?"

"In three days."

I thought, what a goddam case! I was about to ask some more questions when three of the Brothers came up to us. They looked unpleasant.

One said: "We have asked you not to come to the Vineyard, Mr McGee."

"This is a public day," McGee said.

"Yes, but we do not care to have you in the grounds."

"Are you going to put me out?"

"If necessary, Mr McGee."

McGee got off the bench.

"Let's go," I said.

"No." McGee glared at the three Brothers. "I believe you are incorporated as a religious institution."

They stared at him, not answering.

"You see," McGee said triumphantly to me. "They don't know." He turned to them. "I'll inform you. You are so incorporated. And the law reads that such incorporated property is open to those who wish to worship."

One of the Brothers had red hair. He said: "You are not here to worship."

More of the Brethren were collecting. A half a dozen were moving in on us. "Let's go," I said.

"You don't know whether in my heart I worship or not," McGee said to the red-headed man.

"You will please go."

Several of the Brothers moved close to McGee. "So much as touch a finger to me," he said, "and I will bring suit."

"Will you leave?" the red-headed man asked grimly.

"In my good time," said McGee.

More were coming. Suddenly I noticed one was the dark man I'd knocked out in the women's building the time I'd first seen Penelope Grayson. He recognized me at the same moment. He nudged the man next to him and whispered something, and they both scowled at me.

"For God's sake," I said to McGee, "let's go."

He was having a fine time. He bowed to the red-headed man. "I leave now, but only of my own free will." He smiled at him. "Do you understand?"

The man didn't reply. We went to the touring car, followed by my dark friend, the red-headed man and twenty other Brothers. The line was still waiting on the mausoleum steps, and cars were still coming up the driveway. A lot of people were rubbering at us. We got in the car. McGee started the engine and waved to the Brothers. "Giddap," he said, and we drove away.

I turned back. The Brothers were still watching us. "They don't seem to care for you," I said to McGee.

"I don't care for them either," McGee said, swinging the car on to the main highway. "Do you know what I once did?"

"No."

"Well, the Vineyard doesn't own any of the places it operates. Never has. I came into some money, so I bought half a dozen of the places, thinking I could force the Vineyard out. I raised the rents a hundred per cent."

"Well?"

"The Vineyard met the raise without a holler."

CHAPTER 13

McGee let me off at the Arkady and I went down to the Turkish bath. I intended to steam out some brandy, but first I had to tend to my gut. It seemed to me I was hungry all the time now. I had the Finn send for a double tenderloin steak, french fries, two orders of sliced tomatoes, bread, coffee and half an apple pie. I read the paper while I waited.

I got a laugh right away. A man hunt was going on in the county, and the man was Peter Jensen, of Fond du lac, Wisconsin. Me! What had happened was this: the cops discovered the car that crashed into Papas's cabin had been rented from the Drive-It by a Peter Jensen. He had reported it stolen, but this, the cops said, was a trick to throw them off the track. The theory now was the shooting at Papas's had been an attempted hold-up, with Jensen the brains behind it. The paper called him a mystery man.

That was fine. I liked being a mystery man. It wasn't such a hell of a distinction, though. I'd never heard of a big police case that didn't have a mystery man or, better, a mystery woman. Usually she was a woman in a black veil. The cops had to have their romance. I got up and went to the toilet. I took the card identifying me as Peter Jensen out of my wallet and tore it up and dropped it in the water. Then I pulled the chain. "So long, Pete," I said.

I went back and looked at the paper again. The hood I'd killed had been identified as Piper Sommes. He had worked in one of the town's pool halls. The cops said he was one of the stick-up mob under Jensen. Nothing was said to link him with Pug Banta. Another body was identified as Joe Manno, one of Papas's waiters. They still had one corpse to go. A trace had been found of Gus Papas. A car with five Greeks in it had gassed up at a filling station in Cairo, Illinois. One of them was wounded. The attendant had reported the wounded man to the local sheriff. It was thought they were heading for Chicago.

It *was* Papas, I decided. He was probably clearing out for good. Greeks never liked fighting. I wondered what had happened to Winnie and the two men. They'd probably decided to keep quiet. I had an idea one of the men had been cheating with Winnie. I read some more. I was reading Chief Piper's statement that Caryle Waterman had been killed accidentally during the stick-up, when a waiter came with my food. I put the paper down. Upstairs someone had figured there were two of us, and the waiter set two places on the rubbing table. That was all right with me. It meant I got twice as much bread and coffee.

When I finished the pie I told the Finn to send the dishes up to the kitchen. I got undressed and took the paper and a towel into the steam room. I would steam for half an hour, and then I would take a rub and a cold shower. Then I'd go about my business. I wanted to do something about Oke Johnson. I felt guilty about him.

I sat on the wooden bench and tried to find something in the paper about Oke. I couldn't. The Papas job had made the shooting unimportant. I read a statement by the DA saying he was going to clean up the county. There was another statement by the mayor. And another by the

Governor. The lid was off. I hadn't done so badly. It was a break, getting Caryle Waterman killed. On an inside page I saw a picture of the burned cabin. There wasn't anything left but the foundation and the stone fireplace.

It was hard to read because the steam blurred the print. I put the paper down and sat without looking at anything much. The steam was so thick I couldn't see the opposite wall, anyway. Waves of it kept rising from the pipes, warm and smelling of menthol. Sweat ran off my face and chest, tickling my skin. I wondered if I was losing weight. I thought about Ginger, wondering how she would look in the steam room. I thought about her long legs and high breasts. I didn't get much of a buzz from it. The Princess had fixed that. I wouldn't have gotten a buzz from George White's chorus.

I tried to think about business. I had two days to get the Grayson girl. I wondered why McGee didn't come through. A lawyer usually knew of a way to do anything. I wiped my face with the towel and then I got a handful of salt out of the box and gave myself a rub down with it. The salt stung, but it cleaned my skin. I was still sweating. I began to relax. The menthol made the steam feel good in my lungs.

The worst was the Ceremony of the Bride. It sounded theatrical, but everything sounded that way at the Vineyard. Still, I didn't like the idea of there being no surviving brides. What if the brides just disappeared after the ceremony? Were sent away, or something? That didn't sound possible. People don't disappear. They write to their families, or send for clothes, or draw out money in banks. But if they died, like McGee said, how could the Vineyard keep it a secret?

I asked that last question, but it was just a formality. I knew almost anything could be kept a secret at the Vineyard. Religious cults were the hardest nuts of all to crack. Look at Father ——, for instance. The Government's been trying for years to find out where he gets the dough to ride in Rolls-Royces and buy estates on the Hudson, but he doesn't even bother to file an income tax. It wouldn't be too tough for the Vineyard to get rid of a girl a year. They could say she had gone away and nobody would be wiser, just so the body didn't turn up.

It was all probably phony; girls didn't get killed that way, but it scared me. It would be the end if Penelope Grayson disappeared. I could see myself explaining to Grayson that I thought she was dead, but I didn't know where the body was. He would like that! I was in a tough spot with a lot of very strange people, and I had three days to get out of it. I began to think about how it would be to live in Mexico. I had nearly four grand. That would last for a while. The trouble was they didn't have many redheads in Mexico.

Someone opened the door. I felt the steam move with the draught. I couldn't see across the room.

"Craven?"

"Yes."

I didn't recognize the voice. It wasn't the Finn. The door closed and the mist didn't drift any more. I couldn't see anything through the steam.

"God damn you, Craven," the voice said. "You killed my sister."

I rolled off the bench to the floor. The pistol made kind of a *plop* and lead flattened against the tile wall over me. Brother, that was one time I was plenty scared. I couldn't think who was shooting at me, or what he was talking about. I didn't know anybody's sister. I crawled towards the shower booth that people used to wash off the salt. He fired again. Now I could barely see something dark through the steam, but I knew he couldn't see as much of me. My skin was closer to the colour of the steam, especially right now.

I said: "Get back or I'll shoot."

"Don't kid me."

He started forward. I picked up the wooden box of salt and threw it at him. It caught him high up and he went back out of sight against the door. I heard him hit the door. I got to my feet and started to rush him and my feet slipped on the wet floor. I hit my jaw a hell of a crack on the table. I hurt my knees and elbows. I crawled to the shower booth. He fired twice. Neither shot came near me. I crawled into the stall, expecting a shot in the backside.

I was glad to get in that stall. It was a funny feeling, being naked and fighting a man with a gun. I didn't like it. I felt the bullets would hurt more, naked. I ran my hands around the stall and found a bar of soap and a back brush. They made a really fine pair of weapons. I couldn't see the guy. He was quiet now, waiting for me to move. He'd shot four times. That left two or three bullets. That was nothing to be cheerful about. It would only take one to knock me off.

I peeped around a corner of the stall. The steam was so thick I couldn't see him. I wondered if the Finn had heard the shots. I wondered if the steam in the room had muffled them. Then I saw him! He was coming slowly towards me. He didn't know where I was, but he was going to get up close for his last shots. I watched him come, seeing his clothes through the steam.

I waited a second, and then I shook the shower curtain. He fired twice; I felt the curtain twitch as the bullets went through it. I knelt and groaned a couple of times, made a gasping noise in my throat, and then held my breath. He was a sucker. He came right up to the curtain. I reached out and jerked his legs. The pistol went off as he fell. He lit hard, and I crawled up and wrestled away the pistol. He didn't have much fight, but I socked him twice with the pistol. He lay still on the floor.

I still didn't know who he was. I didn't wait to find out. I ran out of the steam room. The Finn was standing by the door looking wild.

"What's the matter?" he asked.

"Nothing." I got a fifty-dollar bill out of my wallet. "Get a hammer and some nails." He hesitated and I shoved the fifty at him. His eyes bulged out. He got the hammer and the nails. "Be fixing something," I said.

He looked around the room. "What'll I fix?"

I picked up a chair and jerked the back off it. "Here."

He began to work on it, pounding hard. I hid the pistol under a towel, and then I sat on the rubbing table and began to talk. "There they were with sixty seconds to play," I said, "and Duke leading three to nothing, and me with one hundred smackers on California. So what do I do? I say to Fritz: 'I'll pay the bet off fifty cents on the dollar.' And Fritz says 'Okay'."

I looked up, very surprised, as the room clerk and a uniformed cop came running into the room. They stopped when they saw the Finn hammering at the chair.

"What's this?" I said.

The clerk turned to me. "Oh, Mr Craven." He giggled. "The awfullest thing. I thought I heard shots down here."

"We didn't hear 'em," I said, looking at the Finn. "I guess he's been making too much noise."

The Finn pounded in a nail. The clerk giggled. The policeman snorted and said: "And me eating my lunch." They went out. I slid off the table and went into the steam room.

I had been scared to death he was going to come to while the cop was around, but I needn't have worried. He was still out, lying on the stone floor just where I left him. I went over and looked down at him. At first I didn't recognize him, and then I did. It was the punk who had brought me the message from Carmel. The one who'd sat at the coffee-shop counter with me. His face was white and pinched-looking. I didn't know if the steam made him look that way, or the knock on the head. I hauled him out of the steam room. The Finn took off his clothes and I stuck him under a cold shower. That brought him around. He spluttered and gasped, trying to get his breath. He was a little guy, not over a hundred and thirty pounds, and very thin. I could see his ribs. I tossed him a towel.

"Now, what's the great idea?" I asked.

The punk looked scared, but he said: "There isn't any."

"You took those shots at me just for the hell of it?"

"No."

"Well, then; why?"

The punk didn't answer, just stood by the shower with the towel draped around him. I saw this wasn't getting me very far.

"What makes you think your sister's dead?" I asked.

He wouldn't say.

"Look," I said. "I wouldn't kill her. She was a friend. I liked her."

He stared at me for a minute, still angry, and then he began to cry. "She was all I had," he gasped between sobs. I thought, well, for God's sake! I called to the Finn and told him to get us a couple of drinks. The punk cried, leaning against the wall, holding the towel around him, until the drinks came. The Finn had gotten rye with ginger ale. I made the punk drink his. After a while he stopped crying.

"Now tell me about it," I said.

It took quite a while to get him talking. I showed him a card that said I was a special investigator for the Treasury Department, but what really did it was my not being sore because he'd tried to kill me. He said he guessed he had been mistaken. He said he was sorry.

"What makes you think your sister's dead?" I asked again.

"I know." He began to breathe hard. "I saw her body."

"The hell!" I yelled for the Finn. "Bring the bottle this time," I told him.

The Finn went for the rye. "Where'd you see her?" I asked the kid.

"She's—her body's—at an undertaker's in Valley."

I remembered something I'd seen in the paper. I went into the steam room and brought out the paper. It was wet, but the print hadn't smeared. I found the story I was thinking about on page six.

> Valley, Aug 10.—The nearly nude body of a young woman, presumably beaten to death, was found early today in a ditch by the Daniel Boone Pike. A pretty brunette about twenty-five years old, she had no marks of identification on her. She was clad only in silk stockings and underclothes. It is believed she was thrown from a passing car.

Valley was a village about sixty miles towards St Louis from Paulton. It was a couple of counties away. I showed the item to the punk.

"Yes."

"What a bad break," I said.

I thought it *was* a bad break. She had been a nice little whore, and she had helped me. *She had helped me!* I began to feel creepy.

"How did you link me with her?" I asked.

"They told me at the house you were looking for her yesterday . . . pretty sore about something." The punk was crying. "So I added two and two."

"And got six," I said.

"Maybe."

"Absolutely," I said. "I'm doing a job of work here." I flashed the Treasury card at him again. "I wasn't sore at her. I was sore because they wouldn't tell me where she was."

"The Negro girl wouldn't?"

"Nobody would. So I got sore. You see the wreckage?"

The punk nodded.

"Well," I said, "I finally found she'd gone out with . . . somebody."

He'd stopped crying. "Who?"

"First you do some talking."

"All right."

The Finn came with the bottle of rye. I poured a good slug in the punk's glass. "Drink." He gulped it down.

"How'd you find she was in Valley?" I asked. He shook his head, and I asked: "Do you want me to turn you in?"

"I don't care."

"Attempted murder's a tough rap. Come on. Who told you?"

"Ginger," he said. "She called me up. Yesterday afternoon. I wouldn't believe her. But she said to go to Valley. 'Just go,' she said. So I did."

"Did Ginger mention me?"

"No." He shook his head, thinking. "But when I told them at the house they said it must have been you."

"They would say that. But why did you think I'd killed Carmel?"

"I don't know."

"Did Ginger say how she knew where she was?"

"No."

I poured us both some rye. I drank mine and filled the glass again. "At the house," I said, "they told me she'd gone with Chief Piper."

"So that's . . ." the kid began.

"Wait a second. Ginger's a friend of Pug Banta's. And so's the chief. But Ginger isn't a friend of the chief. Can you add that up?"

"No."

"It's not so tough." I took a drink of the rye. "Pug thought Carmel had spilled some dope to me. And he knew she wouldn't come out to meet him."

He nodded his head. "That's right."

"So he got Chief Piper to call her. And when she came, Pug took her."

"Yeah?" He was a little doubtful.

"Sure. And after he killed her, he gave it away to Ginger. Maybe by accident. And she called you, being sorry for your sister."

I took a shower while he thought this over. The sweat from the steam room had begun to get sticky. I decided to forget the rub down. I wanted to go where I could do some heavy thinking. It seemed to me things were a little out of control. The poor goddam whore! At that, maybe she was better off dead. When I came out, the punk was putting on his clothes.

"Where're you going?"

"To find Pug."

"That's no good. Pug's too tough. Besides, we don't know for sure if he did it."

"I know."

"Just a little while ago you thought it was me."

That stopped him.

"Have you claimed her yet?"

"No."

"Do that first. Give me some time to look around. I'll work out something. Where do you want to have her buried?"

"At home, I guess."

"Where's that?"

"Temple."

Temple was another little town about a hundred miles the other way from Valley. "You got the dough?" I asked.

"I don't know."

"Here." I got a couple of hundreds out of my wallet. "This will help. Let me know what you do."

"Well, thanks. . . ."

"Forget it," I said.

I took a cab down to the red-brick County Building and went up to the second floor where the records were kept. Half drawn blue blinds made the record room gloomy. An old clerk with thin white hair and the palsy got me the records I wanted. It looked as though McGee had told me the truth. *Tony's* was owned by Thomas McGee. So was the *Arkady Hotel*. And the *Silver Grove*, a dance hall. And the *Ship*, Paulton's only cabaret.

"One more," I told the old clerk. "Five hundred and sixty-nine Green Street."

That was the whorehouse. He brought me the papers. The owner was Thomas McGee.

At the hotel there was a message from Western Union. They had the money order. I went down and identified myself and the girl gave me a cheque for a thousand. I had her call the bank, and then I went around and cashed the cheque. That gave me more than five thousand in cash. I felt like getting drunk.

Instead I went to a jewellery store just off Main Street. "Something nice for a lady," I told the salesman.

"What sort of a present?" he asked. "A bracelet?"

"Sure," I said.

He pulled out a tray of bracelets and put it on the glass counter. They looked cheap. There was a lot of gold and coloured glass and fake diamonds. "How much?"

"They range from five to twenty-five."

"Oh, hell! Something fancier than that."

He brought out another tray. The stuff didn't look much

better. The clerk was fat, and sweat ran off his face. It made me hot to look at him. I wiped my face with a handkerchief.

"Now this one is nice," he said, holding up one with big gold links. "Solid gold."

In another part of the showcase I saw a honey. It was wide, and it was made of what looked like diamonds and square-cut sapphires. I pointed at it.

"How much?"

"Seventy-five. It's a very fine imitation."

"Wrap it up."

I counted out the money. Then I got a card and wrote: "Baby, why be sore at me?"

I took the parcel and went back to the hotel. I gave the parcel to the giggly desk clerk.

"Give this to Ginger."

"I certainly will, Mr Craven," he said. "The very minute she comes in."

CHAPTER 14

IN THE lobby I found the card on which I'd written the name of Oke Johnson's friend. *Carter Jeliff.* I looked him up in the phone book. He was a butcher, and he lived at 987 Oak Street. I thought Carter Jeliff was a flossy name for a butcher.

I got a cab and rode out to Oak Street. It was hot outdoors, but big trees shaded the street. There were cool places under the trees. I wondered about Jeliff. Oke Johnson was a sour bastard; he didn't make friends with anybody unless there was something in it for him. I didn't see why he'd be fooling around with a butcher.

I told the driver to wait. Mrs Jeliff came to the door. "He's in the garden," she said.

Jeliff looked the way all butchers should look. He was big, almost as big as me, but not so tall, and he had a face like a ham. He was a blond. He was watering some tomato vines. I told him my name and said I was a friend of Oke Johnson's. He said he was glad to see me, and wasn't it too bad about poor Oke? I said it was.

He turned off the water and asked me if I'd like a beer. I said sure. We went down in the cellar. It was dark and cool. He got two quart bottles of beer out of a washtub and opened them.

"This is where I spend Sunday," he said.

There were at least two dozen quarts of beer in the tub, and a cake of ice. I wondered if he drank them all himself. He said *Prosit!* and we drank, sitting in a couple of wicker chairs.

He didn't look like a guy you could buy information from; he looked honest. I told him I was a private detective. I told him I was interested in Oke Johnson's death. Was there anything he knew about it?

He grinned at me. "Do you think I did it?"

"Hell, no. I just found out he was friendly with you. That's all."

He said that relieved him. He chuckled a little at his joke. Then he got serious. He said he'd noticed one thing. "Oke was nervous about something."

"What?"

"He never told me. But I knew. He was afraid of strangers, and one night he said he thought he was being followed."

"Was he?"

"I don't know."

"Did he ever tell you what he was doing?"

"No."

This didn't seem to be going anywhere. We had two more bottles of beer while I tried more questions. I began to feel fine; the beer and the cellar were so cool.

"Look," I said. "Oke wasn't a very friendly guy."

"He seemed friendly enough to me."

"Maybe because he wanted to get something out of you."

He thought that over. "That's a blow," he said, grinning.

"Did he ever question you about anything?"

"Only about the butcher business."

The hell! I thought. The butcher business. That had a lot to do with a murder case. I kept on, though.

"In what way?" I asked.

"Well!" He thought for a minute. "He seemed to be interested in the meat I sell the Vineyard."

"You supply them?"

"No. I just sell 'em left-overs. Anything I can't use. They pay a good price, too."

I began to get excited. "Who pays you for 'em?"

"Brother Joseph."

That was why Oke had been friendly with Jeliff. Meat for the Vineyard. I had hit on something. I felt good until I had another thought: Why was Oke interested in the meat?

Jeliff didn't know the answer. All he knew was he delivered meat to Brother Joseph at the Elder's house once a week. It didn't matter how badly spoiled it was; Brother Joseph paid for it just the same.

"If they're crazy out there," he asked, "should I care?"

I finished the beer and thanked him and said goodbye. It felt twice as hot outside after being in the cellar. I got in the cab. All the way back to the hotel I tried to figure why Oke had been interested in the meat delivered to the Vineyard. I didn't get the answer.

I had a four-pound steak for lunch. I couldn't seem to get enough meat. My system craved it all the time. Rare meat. I had it served in my room. For some reason I didn't feel comfortable outside. I ate the steak lying down.

When the waiter took away the table, I stayed on the bed and read *Black Mask*. My belly was full of meat. A hot wind blew in the window and I began to sweat. I felt tired again. I thought back and figured I'd had seven hours' sleep in the last three days. I decided a bath and a nap would do me good. I got up and undressed. I found myself ducking every time I passed the windows. I peeked out. They looked down on Main Street, and there were no tall buildings near. No guy would shoot at me from Main Street. Just the same I pulled the curtains.

I filled the tub with cold water and lay in it for a long time. I thought it was funny I should be spooky. Maybe it was the kid trying to shoot me. I'd never feel good in a steam room again. I tried to think about the Vineyard's meat. Slightly decayed meat. What the hell would anybody want that for?

I thought about the Princess. Maybe she could tell me about the meat. I was to see her again tonight. It was to be a regular nightly custom. Well, it was a great experience. I wondered how long I could stand up under it. Maybe some night I . . .

I heard somebody in the room; feet and the sound of the door closing. I turned my neck, but I couldn't see into the room. The bathroom door was nearly shut. I wished I'd bought another revolver. If I got through this, I would.

"Who's there?" I called.

The feet came towards the bathroom. The door opened a little and I got ready to jump out of the tub. Ginger stuck her head through the opening, smiling.

"Hello," she said.

She looked nice with her white skin and red hair. I pulled a towel off the rack and put it over me like an apron. "What the hell!" I said. "I'm taking a bath."

"I've seen naked men before," Ginger said.

"Not like me."

"Maybe," she admitted. She came in the bathroom and sat on a shower stool.

I had to laugh. "Why don't you take off your clothes and get in with me?"

"There wouldn't be room."

"I'll make room."

"I bet."

"Then come on."

"No, thanks." Her face got serious. "I came to talk about the bracelet."

"Oh. How'd you like it?"

"It's beautiful. How much did it cost?"

"Plenty."

"You're not a bad guy." She twisted the bracelet on her arm. It looked fine with the black long-sleeved dress she had on. The fake diamonds gleamed in the bathroom light.

"Listen, you shouldn't have given it to me. Pug Banta's got it in for you, anyway."

"Yeah?"

"He found out Carmel gave you the dope on him."

"Yeah. From Carmel . . . before he killed her."

Her eyes got wide. "How'd you know she was dead?"

"Her brother told me."

"The poor gal." She shook her head at me. "And you're probably next."

"Not me. He knows killing me'll get him in trouble with the Vineyard."

"He's getting so he doesn't care," Ginger said. She leaned over the tub. "Look. Why don't you beat it? He doesn't know where you live. He'd never find you. And you won't have to pay for a coffin then."

"Did he send you here to tell me that?"

"Why, you fool!" Her green eyes got hard. She took a breath. "If you aren't the most conceited bastard! Pug isn't scared of anyone."

"That's what you think."

"I suppose he's scared of you."

"He's not smart enough to be," I said. "But ask him about the Princess sometime."

That made her mad. I could see it in her eyes. "I'm sick and tired of hearing about the Princess."

"What's the matter," I said, "can't you compete with her?"

She got off the stool. "I'll slug you!" She pulled off the bracelet. "Here!" She threw the bracelet in the tub. "You know where you can stick that, you louse!"

"Thanks."

"And, brother, don't say I didn't warn you when Pug gets you."

She started for the door. I fished around in the tub for the bracelet. "Don't go away mad," I said.

"I'm not mad. I never get mad."

I heard her close the door. I got another towel and dried off the bracelet. I threw the wet towel on the tile floor. Water oozed out of it. I felt better. Seeing Ginger had made me feel better. I got a drink and lay naked on the bed. I thought about Ginger, and then I thought about the Princess.

It was three o'clock. I had four hours before I was due at the Vineyard. I already had that funny feeling in my stomach. I took a big drink of rye and cold water and then lay on the bed. The Princess was the best for one thing I'd ever had. She was as good as any whore in the world, and her heart and soul were in her work. She had a beautiful body, steel and silk and marble and rubber all rolled in one. I felt the excitement grow. I took another drink, and then I got in the shower. I let the cold water run over me. I soaked a sheet in the water and got in bed without drying myself and pulled the wet sheet over me. It was cooler that way. I got up and locked the door. I went back to bed and in a little while I fell asleep. I was really sore when the clerk woke me by telephone at six-thirty, but another shower and a drink cleared my head. I wondered what the Princess would have for dinner.

CHAPTER 15

I WOKE with a start, my heart up where my Adam's apple should have been. I found I was having trouble breathing. Moonlight blinded my eyes. I smelled a woman, but I didn't know who it was. I didn't even know where I was. For a minute I thought I was back with the first woman I'd ever slept in bed with, the physical ed. teacher at Lincoln High while I was a junior there. It was confusing to think that.

When my eyes got used to the light I saw a woman by the bed. She was staring down at me. I saw her body through her silk nightie, and I remembered everything. It was the Princess. She had been watching me while I was asleep. I sat up, feeling spooked, and stared back at her. Her skin looked milky in the moonlight. The pupils of her eyes were dark and uneven, like splotches of ink. Her face was strange.

She whispered: "How much guts have you, honey?"

Everything seemed unreal. I felt as though I was dreaming. The moonlight had changed the look of the room, made things stand out I'd never noticed before. An open closet door threw a tall shadow on the wall. The foot of the bed looked like a picket fence. There was a second moon in a mirror. I still had trouble breathing.

She whispered again: "Honey, how much?"

"God damn you," I said. "Did you wake me up just to ask me that?"

She put her hand on my bare chest. Her skin was hot. "How would you like fifty grand?"

I was awake now. "Where is it?"

"In the temple."

She sat on the edge of the bed, leaving her hand on my chest. There was a vault in the temple, she said; in the basement. In it were the gifts people had made to the Vineyard for years; jewellery, ornaments, gold and silver . . . and money.

"They don't keep any records," she said. "Nobody knows how much is there. What we take won't be missed."

"Why haven't you taken it long ago?"

"I needed help," she said. "There was nobody I could trust."

"What makes you think you can trust me?"

"I can as long as Pug Banta's alive."

I thought that over. She was right. I would be finished if she turned me up to Pug. He wanted to get me bad enough, but so far she had stood in the way.

She said: "Are you coming?"

"This way? Naked?"

She went to the dresser and got out one of the Vineyard's costumes. There was a white silk blouse and black trousers. I put them on. The trousers were tight around the waist. She put on a red robe. While she was fastening it, I found the brandy decanter and had a drink.

"What's the routine?" I asked.

"Not so loud." She came close to me. "There's one guard at the door," she whispered. "We get rid of him, and then everything's jake."

"Isn't the door locked?"

"I've got a duplicate key."

"It doesn't sound bad," I said. "Only how will we get rid of the guard?"

"You'll have to kill him."

She said this as though she was saying I should have another drink. I stared at her. The moonlight showed no expression at all on her face. She was pale and calm. Her eyes were like black pools of water, the pupils were so big. I began to get that feeling of being in a dream again.

"Listen," I said. "We're not killing anybody."

"We'll make it look like an accident."

"No," I said.

She saw I meant it. "All right. We can get him out of the way. I can."

"You're not fooling?"

"I do think it's safer to kill him."

"I won't go for murder, and that's final."

"Come on, then." Her voice was scornful. She pushed me towards the door.

"Don't we wear shoes?"

She gave me another push. We went out the hall and through the back door and around the women's building, all the time walking in the shadows. The grass was wet with dew. It felt cool underfoot. From the look of the moon I figured it was about two o'clock. The buildings were all dark. Everybody was asleep. We walked back of some bushes towards the temple. I padded along silently in my bare feet.

The temple was white in the moonlight, its shape smooth and round like a cake. It looked very big. I saw lights flickering behind one of the stained-glass windows. There was a woman on the window, the Virgin, I guess; and the lights made her look as though she was shaking her head at us. It gave me a hell of a start. I pointed the lights out to the Princess.

"Candles," she whispered. "They burn all the time."

We went around to the back of the temple. A bat flew a couple of times at my white shirt. I stumbled over a sprinkler. The Princess came to a door and halted. She listened at the door, then turned to me.

"You'll have to tie up the guard," she whispered.

"What with?"

She handed me some silk cord; the kind she wore around her waist to keep her robe together. I tried to break it but I couldn't. "Okay," I said.

She opened the door. At the far end of a long room I saw light faintly reflected. I couldn't see what made the light. She closed the door and we went down five stone steps. The stone was cold on my feet. We walked along a stone floor towards the light, moving slowly. I smelled an odour of decay, not strong, but very plain. It reminded me of the stink around the Kansas City stockyards. I thought it was probably old Solomon upstairs, turning over in his coffin.

At the end of the room was another door. This one was open. I saw now the reflected light was flickering a little. It came from a candle. The Princess looked around the door, and then touched my hand. Her fingers felt feverish. I moved forward. I saw a man in a costume like mine sitting by a padlocked door. There was a candle burning on the stone floor by his chair, the yellow flame looking thin in all the darkness. The man was asleep, his chin resting on his chest. He had bushy black hair. The Princess nudged me forward.

I got about half way to the man when he woke up. He blinked his eyes at me, still half asleep. "Who is it?"

I walked slowly so as not to scare him. He looked at me, trying to see who I was. He had a big round face and heavy eyebrows. He didn't get alarmed until he noticed I hadn't any shoes. Then he stood up, and I jumped him. We went down together, splintering the chair under us. He fought hard, but I was stronger. I got my hands on his throat and began to choke him, pushing my thumbs into the muscles under his jaw. He kicked in agony and the candle went out. I held him down with my weight, feeling his breath rattle under my palms. Suddenly he went limp and I let go of his throat.

"Are you all right, honey?" the Princess whispered.

"Yes."

I went through the man's pockets and found a packet of matches. I lit the candle. The light showed the Princess standing by the man, staring down at him. "Did you kill him?"

"Hell, no!"

She looked at me as though she'd never seen me before. She watched me tie his hands and feet and gag him with his undershirt. Her eyes were strange, as though she was in a trance. She gave me a key. "For the padlock."

I left her looking down at him and went to the door. The key wasn't a very good fit. It turned hard, but I got it around. The lock came open. I took it off the hasp and shoved open the door.

Inside it looked like a junk shop. There were chests and tables and piles of paintings and vases and books and statues, and God knows what else, all jumbled together on the floor. Near the door I saw a silver candelabra with two candles. I lit the candles and went into the room.

It looked more like a junk shop than ever. There were hundreds of things in the room. The candlelight shone off a silver tea-set and some silver platters in a corner. Next to these was a small gold-framed picture of a woman's head. She had her hair parted in the middle and hung in two braids over her shoulders. On a red Chinese chest were some gold salt shakers. I almost stepped on some kind of a tapestry showing men hunting a boar in a forest. There was a sword with a jewelled hilt leaning against a bronze statue of a naked boy. I saw the name Scott engraved on the sword. Under a table was a whole set of hand-painted china, including a couple of huge platters, and on the table was a clock with the four seasons, the sun and the moon and the hours all on separate dials. I saw a hand-carved model of a frigate, a big pipe with a silver bowl, a spinning-wheel, an Oriental rug, an engraved silver bit for a horse, an inkwell made from jade.

This wasn't a fiftieth part of the junk. I was still staring at the things when the Princess came into the room. She was breathing so hard I turned around to look at her. Her face was calm; only her chest moved with her quick breaths. Her eyes went around the room.

"Has he come to yet?" I asked.

"No." Her voice sounded flat and lifeless.

"He'll be all right," I said.

She nodded, but I don't think she paid any attention to what I said. She was looking at the room.

"Where'd all this come from?" I asked.

"The Brothers and Daughters," she said. "They have to take vows of personal poverty when they enter the Vineyard. They turn everything over to the Elders."

I stared at the mess of stuff. "God, what junk!"

"You don't think it's any good?"

"Do you?"

She opened one of the chests. "Look." I held the candelabra over the chest. It was full of watches: gold watches, silver watches, men's watches, women's watches, watches with jewels on the covers, engraved watches. "My God!" There were probably five or six hundred watches there.

She opened another chest. This was full of necklaces and bracelets. The stones gleamed in the light. A lot of them were cheap-looking, but some looked wonderful. I saw one, a kind of collar, that must have had a hundred diamonds in it. The next chest was filled with rings and cameos. Another was full of loose jewels. They were mostly semi-precious stones, but I saw diamonds sparkling in the heap. I put my hand in this chest and felt the stones. They were slick and cold.

"Pick out some of the diamonds."

I put the candelabra down and got a couple of dozen fairly good-sized diamonds out of the chest. One was about five carats, and none was under two. They glittered in the soft light.

The Princess closed the chest. She took the diamonds away from me. "Now for the dough," she said.

She went to a small table at the back of the room, the one with the fancy clock on it, and opened the drawer. Brother, my eyes fairly popped out of my head! The drawer was full of paper money. There were hundreds of bills, many of the old size. These looked strange, bigger than I'd remembered them. She put her hands in the bills, feeling with her fingers for something. She brought her hands out filled with gold pieces. Their colour was a dull yellow in the light of the candles. They made a soft clinking noise. I took one from her and felt it. It was heavy. It was like finding a mine. I picked up a handful of paper money. I had hold of twenties, and fifties, and hundred-dollar bills, and three one-thousand-dollar bills. I had four or five thousand dollars, and it hadn't made a hole in the drawer.

"They turn their cash into big bills," the Princess said, "and give it up along with everything else when they come in."

She began to sort out bills worth a hundred dollars or more. I helped her, digging my hands deep down in the money. There was a lot of gold there, but we didn't touch it. The bills crackled as we sorted them. We worked for a long time. Once I thought I heard a noise. Our shadows seemed to shiver as we listened.

"You're just spooked," the Princess said scornfully.

We counted what we'd taken. There were twenty-five thousand-dollar bills, thirty six-hundred-dollar bills, twenty-four two-hundred-dollar bills, and sixty-three one-hundred dollar bills.

"How much?"

I said it came to fifty-four thousand, one hundred dollars. The Princess started to pick up the money.

"Wait a minute."

"I'll just carry it."

"No, you won't," I said.

I gave her twenty-seven thousand and tossed the extra hundred back in the drawer. I put the rest in my pocket. It made quite a wad of money. "Let's get the hell out of here," I said.

"All right."

We went out the door. The guard was still lying on the floor. I could just see him by the broken chair. I blew out the two candles on the candelabra, and put it in the vault. Then I fastened the padlock. I turned around, and suddenly

I noticed something queer about the guard. He was lying in a strange sprawled-out way. I went over to him. There was blood all around his head, and a deep wound on his temple. Something had almost crushed his head in, a stone or an iron bar. Something heavy.

The Princess stared at me.

"He's dead!" I said.

"Is he?"

"I don't see . . . did you kill him?"

"Oh, no."

I held the candle over my head. In a corner of the room I saw a pile of bricks. There were twenty or thirty bricks, left over from building the temple. I went over and found one with blood on it.

"You lousy bitch," I said.

"All right," she said.

"You'll get us hung for this."

"Don't be dumb."

"You may like hanging," I said.

"Nobody's going to hang," she said.

I was scared as hell. "We've got to get out of here." I started for the outside door.

"Wait." She grabbed my arm. "We can make it look like an accident."

"Don't be a damn fool. The cops'll see through anything we can do."

"There aren't going to be any cops."

She began to talk fast, in a low voice that was almost a whisper: "You fool, the Vineyard will never call the cops. Not even if the Elders think it was murder. They don't like cops."

I thought this over. "How are we going to make it look like an accident?"

She took the candle from me and held it high above her head. I saw the brick walls, with no plaster on them, and the unfinished ceiling. "See those bricks?"

"Yes."

"Suppose some of them fell on him while he was sitting there?"

"They'd bust him good, all right."

"Well . . . ?"

I said: "But the bricks are still in the wall."

"We have to make them fall."

"It'll take a pick."

"Come on."

I knew I was a fool to follow her, but I was stuck. I was an accessory before the fact. That would carry a first-degree rap. I might as well be one after the fact, too. I couldn't do any worse.

She blew out the candle at the door. I felt surprised everything was so peaceful outside. The moonlight was still bright, and there was a breeze blowing from the east. We went from the shadow of the temple to a line of thick bushes. We went past a small pool with water lilies growing in it. The moon was like a smear of silver on the water and some of the lilies were open. They were white. I heard a mousy squeak and saw a couple of bats above the pool. The bats were feeding on night insects.

I followed the Princess up a hill and into a clump of trees. The grass was as soft and thick as a bathmat here, and it was dry. I guess the trees had kept it from the dew. It was very dark under the trees. I banged a toe against something hard and looked down and saw I'd hit a tombstone. We were walking in a graveyard! I saw other tombstones, and felt with my feet the raised sod over the graves. The Princess went to the left, to an open grave. It had been freshly dug, and the shovels and the picks of the gravediggers were still by the side. The Princess picked up one of the picks and gave it to me.

I took it, looking at the open grave. There was something funny about it. Suddenly I knew what it was. It already had a stone. That was strange. I never heard of them putting up the stone until afterwards. I bent over and read the inscription by the light of the moon. It said:

PENELOPE GRAYSON
(1917–1940)
Her Soul Rests With the Lord

It was a little bit like seeing your own name on a tombstone. It was also a hell of a lot like a very bad nightmare. I blinked at the stone, and then I dropped the pick and grabbed the Princess's arm.

"Is she dead?"

"What do you care?"

"I asked you if she was dead?"

"Not so loud."

"Answer me, or I'll break your goddam neck."

She tried to get loose, and I shook her. She cried out with pain. I shook her again.

"She's not dead," she said.

"Then what's this for?"

"Let me go."

I shook her, my fingers digging into the muscles of her arm. She said: "It's for her after the Ceremony of the Bride."

"They die?"

"Yes." She slipped out of my hands and pointed at some graves by the open one. "Look."

I looked at the stones. Anette Nordstrom (1911–1939); Grace Robins (1913–1938); Tabitha Peck (1920–1937), and Mary Jane Bronson (1910–1936). All young, and all dying in order: 1936, '37, '38, '39, and now '40. I looked again at Tabitha Peck. The poor kid was only seventeen. That was a funny name, Tabitha.

"Now you know all about it," the Princess said. "Come on."

I got the pick. We went back to the temple. She lit the candle. He was lying just where we'd left him. I started to work on the wall, making as little noise as possible. The bricks came out easily.

I'd made quite a hole in the wall and the ceiling by the time my hands began to hurt. I rested for a minute. I was sweating hard. I wiped my face on the sleeve of my blouse. The Princess was standing by the vault door, holding the candle.

"Don't you think that's enough?" she asked.

"We got to make a big pile," I said.

I rested a while, and then I picked up the pick. It felt slippery in my hands. The Princess held up the candle. I saw something glitter in the corner. I went over and picked it up. It was some kind of a metal disk.

"What are you doing?"

"I thought I saw something."

"What?"

"A coin or something." I put the disk in my pocket. "It was just a piece of chipped brick."

"Oh."

I went to work on the wall again.

From the door I looked back at him. I'd brought down so much stuff he was hardly visible. All I could see was a shoe. He was lying on the wrecked chair, just as if he'd been sitting there when the wall fell. There were bricks and plaster all over him, and all over that side of the cellar. It looked as though there'd been an earthquake. It wouldn't fool anyone with any sense, I thought, but it might fool the Brothers. Particularly if they wanted to be fooled. I thought they would be, since the door of the treasure vault was still closed, apparently just as it had always been.

The Princess was standing by the body, holding the candle for me to get to the door. The light made her hair look like spun gold, as they say. I lit a match and she put out the candle and threw it by the body, like we agreed. She walked towards me, coming straight for the burning match. I smelled her when she got to the door, and I began to feel excited. We went outside.

I took the pick back to the hill with the graves, wiped the handle with my blouse, and dropped it by one of the shovels. The open grave looked black and mysterious. The moonlight was coming at such an angle the light didn't reach the bottom. It could have been twenty feet deep. The Princess waited for me at the corner of the temple. We walked back to the women's building, keeping in the shadows.

The moonlight was still pouring into her bedroom, making the bed look big and white. I washed my hands and found the bottle of brandy and had a long drink. It was funny, but I could hardly feel the stuff. I waited a minute, and then I had another drink. My throat felt numb.

She had taken off her robe and got in bed. I sat in a chair and had another drink. I felt her watching me. I had been sweating, and I kept on sweating. I wasn't used to working with a pick. I sat for a long time, drinking and sweating. I took off my blouse. The air felt good on my bare skin.

"Honey," she whispered; "what's the matter?"

"Nothing."

"Come over here with me."

"No."

I had another drink. Then she said: "I'm sorry I killed him."

"This is a hell of a time to be sorry."

"I got frightened, thinking what would happen when he told the Elders. They'd have caught us sure."

"Maybe."

"Oh, yes. We're really better off with him dead."

Her voice was throaty like she had a cold. It made me feel queer. I could see her body under the silk sheet. She hadn't put anything on. I saw the mound her breasts made under the silk, and her hair on the pillow, yellow even in the moonlight.

She whispered: "Honey."

"What?"

"Are you afraid of me?"

"No."

"Then come over. You have to sleep."

I went over, but we didn't sleep.

CHAPTER 16

IN THE morning I caught a street-car into town. The motorman stared at me, but he didn't say anything. It was nine o'clock and the sun was high in a blue sky. I got off at the square and walked to the Arkady. I had the blouse and pants I'd used during the night wrapped in paper, and in the clothes was the dough.

I went up to my room and dumped the money out on the bed. It made quite a heap. Twenty-seven grand! That was more dough than I'd ever seen at one time in my life. I got my knife and made a slit in the under side of the mattress on the spare bed. It was a lousy hiding-place, but it would do for a while. I stuffed twenty thousand dollars through the slit and smoothed out the bed. The rest I put in my pants for pin money.

I pulled the disk I'd found in the temple out of my pocket. It was an American Legion identification tag. It said *Post 23, St Louis*. Below that was a number, 8,834. I wrote out a wire to Legion headquarters in St Louis, asking for the name and address of the Legionnaire with that number. I gave the wire to Charles, the Negro, to send. He rolled his eyes when I told him to keep the change from a ten-dollar bill. Jesus! I felt rich.

At the same time I was plenty scared. I sat on the bed and thought what a jam I was in. It was bad from every angle. I stood at the head of the line for a murder rap, to say nothing of grand larceny, and housebreaking. There were a few other things, too. A very tough gangster was trying to make up his mind whether or not to kill me. My partner had been murdered and I wasn't doing anything about it. I had taken six grand from a client without a chance in hell of doing what I had told him I would do.

I *did* have to get that girl out of the Vineyard. Even if it was only long enough for her to miss the ceremony that was due in two nights now. I thought; it all *must* be phony. It was a human sacrifice; the kind of thing you read about happening in Africa and didn't believe. And here it was in a dopey town almost in the centre of the United States. Things like that didn't happen! Like hell, they didn't! I thought of the Halls-Mills case, the Wyncoop case in Chicago, the case of the two women tourists murdered on the Arizona desert. They happened.

I wondered how the Brides were killed, and who killed them. I wondered if they were slaughtered on Solomon's casket. One of them had been named Tabitha. That was a funny name. The poor kid! Only seventeen!

I looked at my watch. It was ten o'clock. I had a lot to do, only I was pooped. I lay back on the bed and pushed off my shoes. I thought I would nap for an hour.

At one o'clock the phone rang. It was Carmel's brother. He said she was going to be buried at eleven o'clock the next morning at Temple. He seemed to take it for granted I would be there.

"Ginger said she'd come, too."

"Fine," I said. "Have you got a minister?"

"Not yet."

"Get one. I'll pay for him."

"Thanks, Mr Craven."

I hung up, and then I called down for Charles. I wrapped the bracelet in a newspaper and gave it to him. I told him to take it to Ginger.

"Ask her if she'd like to drive me to a funeral tomorrow."

He thought that was a joke.

"No," I said. "Ask her."

It didn't seem like I'd slept at all, so I lay back on the bed again.

The phone rang at three-fifteen.

"Western Union," a man said. "For Karl Craven."

"Okay, Western Union."

"Legionnaire 8,834, is Oscar K. Johnson, 4582 Waverly Street, St Louis. Do you want me to repeat it?"

"No, I got it."

When the phone rang again it was six o'clock. McGee's nasal voice came over the wire. "I want to see you, Craven."

"I'm in bed."

"You'll have to get up. It's very important."

"All right. Are you at your office?"

"Yes. I'll wait for you."

There was a click at the other end. I wondered what had

happened. I went to the bathroom and washed my face, and then I got dressed. The phone rang again.

The Princess said: "Hello, honey."

"Hello," I said.

"Dear, I can't see you tonight."

"No?"

"Are you terribly disappointed?"

"Of course."

"I have to go to the Festival."

I was scared. "My God, is this the night they . . . ?"

"No. Tomorrow night."

"Oh."

"You're not still thinking of getting her out, are you, honey?"

"No," I lied.

"That's a good boy." There was a pause. "What have you done with what we got?"

"It's in a safe place."

"I think it'll be safer together."

"I don't know."

"Yes. Bring it out tomorrow afternoon."

This was a command. "Okay," I said.

"Don't forget, honey; around two tomorrow afternoon."

"I won't."

I hung up. She'd probably decided I was getting too big a cut. I found the bottle of rye and poured myself half a tumblerful. I got my hat and went down the hall to the elevator. When the elevator came I heard a door open up the hall towards my room.

It was hot out on the street. I walked towards town. Near the big movie theatre I stopped in a lunch-counter joint and had three hamburgers, a whole dill pickle and two bottles of beer. Then I had some fresh peach pie. *Strange Cargo* was playing at the movie. A sign said: COOL INSIDE. About a block further down the street I got an idea a man was following me. I looked back and saw a big man in a black suit. I went by McGee's office building and around the block. The man tagged along. I went into the office building.

McGee was sitting at the desk in his private office. He

made washing motions with his hands when he saw me. "You seem to be in trouble, Craven," he said.

"What kind of trouble?"

His eyes watched me out the triangles of flesh. "There has been a robbery at the Vineyard."

"Yeah?"

"Yes. A man was killed and it is believed a sum of money was taken."

"I didn't know they kept any money out there," I said. "How much?"

"The exact sum is not known." He leaned over the desk. "But the point is: they suspect you of having taken it."

"Me?"

"One of the Brothers reported you struck him the other day."

"I did," I said. "But that was so I could talk with the Grayson gal."

He nodded. "I know." He washed his hands again. "But there are other things. You were seen at the Vineyard with me."

I shrugged my shoulders and looked at him. He went on:

"And most important, you were seen leaving the Vineyard early this morning."

"Who saw me?"

"The same Brother."

I wished I had hit his head a little harder, so it had split. "That doesn't look so good," I admitted.

He tapped his fingers on the desk. "Did you take the money?"

"Hell, no."

"You did not kill the guard?"

"I don't know anything about it."

"You're—ah—quite sure?"

"Christ, yes!" I said. "I ought to know who I kill, hadn't I?"

"What were you doing out there last night?"

"Early this morning's more like it," I said. "I wanted to take a look around. I've been thinking I might have to kidnap the Grayson girl, after all."

My story didn't get over so good. "I thought," he said, "we agreed that we wouldn't do that?"

"Well, nothing else seemed to do any good."

"That's true. Quite true." He looked down at his hands. "It is too bad."

"I don't know," I said.

"I don't believe you follow me, Craven. It is too bad it will be necessary for you to leave town."

"Me leave town? Don't make me laugh."

"I am not trying to be funny, Craven. You say you did not steal the money. I believe you."

"That's white of you."

He went right along. "But the Brothers do not. They are very dangerous when aroused. It is not safe for you here."

"I've got to stay."

"I will explain to Mr Grayson," McGee said. "He will not want you to risk your life."

"It's my life."

"They may be after you even now."

"To hell with them."

He stood up. "Well, Craven, I must say I admire your spirit. I hope you will not have to regret your decision."

"Thanks."

"I felt it my duty to warn you."

"Sure."

"If you should change your mind, let me know."

"All right."

He tapped his yellow teeth with a fingernail. "I'd rather you didn't phone me . . . because of the position you're now in. You understand?"

I nodded.

"If it's at night, come to my residence. I read until one in my library. It is in the rear of the house. You can tap at the french doors."

"Okay," I said. "The french doors. But don't count on me coming around."

I went out and after half a block, the guy in the dark suit picked me up again. I began to get creepy. Nobody likes to be followed, especially when it might be somebody with murder in his mind. I thought I'd better find out about the dark suit.

I walked to a place where there was one cab waiting. I got in and said loudly: "To the Arkady." When I got there I went upstairs to my room, slammed the hall door and then opened it a crack. Pretty soon the elevator stopped at the third floor and the guy came out and went into the room next to mine. I waited a minute, and then I knocked on his door.

"Who is it?"

"The room clerk."

The door came open a foot. I put my shoulder against it and shoved my way into the room. The guy in the dark suit had a pistol pointed at my stomach. I closed the door. The guy looked scared.

"What do you want?"

"That's what I came to ask you."

"I don't want anything."

"You've been tailing me," I said. "Why?"

The hand holding the pistol was kind of shaky. "You're wrong, buddy; I haven't followed anybody."

"Nuts," I said.

I saw the guy was cock-eyed. One eye was looking at the door and the other was looking at me. "If you don't get out, I'll call the operator."

"You're sure you haven't been following me?"

"Of course I'm sure. You must be crazy. I don't even know who you are."

I pretended to be convinced. "I'm sorry, mister. Somebody has been following me. I thought he came in here."

"You thought wrong." The guy was getting cocky. He waved the pistol at me. "You're lucky I didn't plug you, buddy, when you pushed into here."

"I guess I was." I turned to go. There was a Bible on the dresser. I picked it up and threw it. He ducked, and I had the gun before he knew what had happened. I hit him with it, and he went down. I let him sit up, and then I kicked his face. The kick stunned him. I pulled a sheet from the bed, tore off a piece and gagged him. I pulled him up on the bed. After a while he came to.

"Now let's have the story, brother," I said.

He made a noise through the gag, but I didn't want to take it off for fear he'd shout. I got a pencil and a sheet of writing-paper from the desk. When I came back he kicked my stomach with both feet. I lit hard on the floor, most of the breath out of me. He slid across the bed towards the telephone. I caught at his legs, but his hands knocked the phone off the table. It crashed on the floor. He tried to kick me again, but I had his legs. I brought him off the bed to his knees. His fists beat against my head. I punched him in the gut and he doubled up, still on his knees. I could hear a voice saying 'Hello' on the phone. I let him have one on the side of the jaw. It cooled him. I crawled to the phone.

"Hello," the clerk was saying. "Hello."

"Hello," I said. "Can you tell me the right time?"

"Why, yes. It's twenty past seven."

"Thank you."

I hung up. I got a towel and wet it and wiped the blood off the guy's face. The water brought him around. He lay on the floor, on his back, trying to get air through the gag. His gasping sounded awful. I wondered if he was going to die.

He got better in a few minutes. The sound of his breathing died away. He looked up at me from the floor, his eyes wet with pain.

"Sit up."

He sat up. I found the pencil and paper and gave them to him. I asked: "Who hired you to tail me?"

He wrote: "The police." I hit him, and said: "You better come clean, brother." Blood began to seep through the gag.

He wrote: "McGee."

I blinked at that. "McGee, eh! Why did he want me tailed?"

He shook his head. I hit him. He wrote: "McGee wanted to frighten you out of town."

"How much did he pay you to do it?"

He wrote: "$200."

"You're earning it," I said. "Get up on the bed."

He crawled up on the bed. I got a hundred-dollar bill out of my pocket. "Where'd you come from?"

"Kansas City."

I tore the bill. "Listen. I'll give you half of this now, and I'll send half to Kansas City, care of Paul Smith, General Delivery, if you telephone me from there in the morning."

He reached for half the bill. "And if you're still in Paulton tomorrow, I'll kill you, so help me," I said. His eyes got big and I stuck the bill in his hand and went to my room. I locked the door and pulled the shades down and undressed. I looked at his pistol. It was loaded. I took it to bed with me.

CHAPTER 17

THE COUPÉ slid along the cement at a smooth sixty, heading for a bank of heavy clouds that steadily got higher on the horizon. The country was flat and dry-looking, and when the coupé got near the edge of the road dust swirled up. It was hot, but the air smelled of rain. We came to a sign saying: *Temple—one mile.*

Ginger was driving. "If Pug ever hears I took you," she said, "he'll bump me."

There wasn't much I could say to that, so I didn't say anything. Ginger let up on the gas. I heard a rumble of thunder. The black clouds covered half the sky. We went by a long field of corn, and then we came to a row of elms. There was a farmhouse and a white fence, and on the lawn two kids were playing with a collie. Temple had two garages, a general store, a drug store, five service stations, a movie with a sign saying: *Next Saturday—Clark Gable in San Francisco*, and a combination restaurant and pool hall. There were about thirty frame houses in the town.

Ginger said: "Now where?"

The dashboard clock said eleven-ten. "The cemetery, I guess."

"Where's that?"

Two old men were sitting on the porch of the general store. I leaned out the window and asked one of 'em: "Dad, where's the cemetery?"

One of the old men had a drooping moustache. He spat through it at a post. "Which one?"

Ginger said: "Jesus! have you got two?"

"How's that?"

I told the old man we wanted the Pendis funeral. He knew about it. It was at Rock Creek Cemetery. He told us how to get there. It was about a mile from town, along a dirt road.

We could see tombstones in the grass on the side of a hill. There was a winding path into the graveyard, and on it were parked five cars. Ahead, and a little off the path, was a hearse. A sudden breeze made yellow flowers nod in the grass, then died away. Apple trees grew in the graveyard.

"The funeral's drawing good," I said.

"She was always a popular girl," Ginger said.

I looked at her, but there was no particular expression on her face. She drove in back of the other cars. People were standing by the hearse. We got out and went over to them. The punk saw me. He had on a blue suit that was too big for him. "Thanks for coming," he said. He gave me back sixty-five from the two hundred I'd given him. "And thanks for the dough."

"It's okay," I said.

A wind came again, and with it thunder. The preacher started over to where the coffin was by an open grave. I got the wreath out of the rear of the coupé. Ginger walked on with the punk, and all the others followed the preacher, too. When I caught up I saw there were a bunch of young girls in the crowd. They shied away from me, their faces frightened. I thought, what the hell! Then I saw an older woman with them, and I knew the reason. It was the madam and the babes from the whorehouse.

While the preacher was saying what he had to say, it began to rain. The drops of water felt queer. They were warm. They didn't cool anything at all. I looked around the crowd and saw the punk. His face was white and he was crying. He looked as though he was going to be sick. I guess he had loved her. The preacher's voice died away and some yokels began to lower the coffin in the grave. The whores were weeping, all but the madam. She stared at me, her face sullen. She was probably thinking of her radio-phonograph combination.

The coffin reached the bottom of the grave and the men slipped off the ropes. All the women in the crowd were crying now, and some of the men. It made me feel a little tight at the throat. The preacher said a few words more, standing bent over so the warm rain wouldn't hit his face. He finished and some of the people threw flowers in the grave. They began to move away. I took a peek into the grave. Flowers had almost covered the coffin. I thought: there goes $135. It was the first time I'd ever spent that much on a doll without getting something in return.

Ginger grabbed my arm. I followed her eyes back to the cars. Through the rain I saw Pug Banta coming towards us, his arms full of roses. Back of him were a couple of his boys. They came right through the mourners, bumping men and women out of their way. I felt Ginger tremble.

"Dear God!" she said.

Pug came up to the grave and dumped the roses on the other flowers. It was raining hard. He walked over to us, looking like some kind of a monkey with his long arms and short legs. His club foot made him limp.

"Come on," he snarled at us. "You're going with me."

We didn't move. His boys stood looking at us from the grave. Carmel's brother left the preacher by the cars and came towards us.

"Come on," Pug said. "Or I'll bump you right here."

Ginger started to go with him. I pulled her back. "Start shooting," I said. "You got a swell audience."

The crowd was beginning to leave. I heard the noise of the motors being started. I saw the punk over Pug's shoulder. I grabbed Pug and threw him down just as the punk fired. I heard the bullet whine. Pug caught me and pulled me down. We wrestled on the ground. I hit Pug and broke away. One of Pug's men jumped the punk and took away the pistol. He slapped the punk's face. I got off the ground.

"Leave him alone," I said to the hoodlum.

He pointed the pistol at my stomach. "Don't get tough."

The people by the hearse had heard the shot. They were looking back at us. Pug got off the ground and began to brush the dirt off his coat. I helped him. The people thought he had fallen and turned away.

"Bring the kid here," Pug said.

They brought him. He cried and struggled with the men. "Damn you," he said.

"What's the idea, kid?" Pug asked.

I said: "He thinks you killed his sister."

Pug went to the punk. "You got me wrong," he said. "Carmel was a swell doll. Would I be bringing her roses if I'd killed her?"

I said to the punk: "You better pay the minister. We'll have a talk later." I gave him a twenty. He threw it on the ground.

"Why did you pull him down?"

I picked the bill up and gave it to him again. "Go pay the minister."

Ginger said: "Come on."

They started to go away, the punk looking bewildered, but the hoodlum with the pistol stopped them. "How about it, Pug?"

"Let 'em go."

They went towards the hearse. Pug scowled at me. "I don't get it, pal."

"The punk thinks you killed his sister."

"No. Why didn't you let him plug me?"

"I'm your friend."

Pug said: "That's a laugh." He scowled at me. "I want to talk to you."

He moved his head towards some graves further up the hill. I followed him. The two bodyguards stayed by Carmel's grave. The rain was nearly over. It was raining under a blue sky now. We stopped by a tombstone with an angel cut on it. I saw green apples on a tree below us.

Pug said: "Anyway, thanks for what you did."

"Forget it."

"Yeah? If I do can you think of any other reason why I shouldn't bump you off?"

"The Princess."

"The hell with her," Pug said. "She's trying to muscle me out."

"No," I said. "You got her wrong."

"Don't give me that."

"She couldn't muscle you or anybody out. She doesn't run the Vineyard."

"Who does, then?"

"McGee." Pug looked blank, and I added: "The lawyer."

Pug said: "Crap."

"Okay. Don't believe me. But McGee's got it in for you. He didn't like the shooting at Papas's. And killin' Carmel."

"Who told you this?"

"I used to work for McGee . . . up to yesterday."

"Either you're a liar or you . . ."

"Do you want me to prove McGee runs the Vineyard?"

Pug scowled. Then he said: "If you can."

"All right. First I'll show you he owns *Tony's* place. And *The Ship*. And the house where Carmel worked. And the *Silver Grove*. And the *Arkady*."

"The Vineyard owns them," Pug said.

"You wouldn't bet on that, would you?"

Pug squinted at me doubtfully. "Why'd you quit McGee if he's Mr Big?"

"I'll show you that, too."

We rode back with Ginger. Pug drove and Ginger sat in the middle. The bodyguards followed in the other car. We made the hundred miles in an hour and twenty minutes. We killed two chickens, a road-runner, a chipmunk and a black-and-white dog. I didn't think Pug was going to be able to stop the coupé in Paulton, we went so fast, but he did, right in front of the County Building.

"Where are those records?"

"Second floor."

"You wait here, baby," Pug said to Ginger.

She didn't know what was going on. I winked at her, but she looked scared. We went up the stone steps and into the building. The old clerk got out the papers for us. Pug scowled when he saw McGee listed as the owner of all the places I asked for. He named some more: the *Savoy Ballroom,* the *Beachcombers, The Hut, Cecil's Grill.* McGee owned them, too.

At the Arkady I had Pug come in with me. "Any calls for me?" I asked the clerk.

The clerk saw Pug, and for once he didn't giggle. "There's a long-distance call from Kansas City, Mr Craven."

While we waited for the call, I told Pug about the guy McGee had hired to tail me. The clerk put the call on an extension in the manager's office. I picked up the receiver. "Hello."

"Well, I've done what you told me, Mr Craven."

"Listen, Kansas City," I said; "there's a fella here I want you to tell what you told me last night. Who paid you, and what he wanted you to do. Wait a second."

I gave the phone to Pug. He listened, asked a couple of questions and then turned to me. "Anything you want to say?"

"Tell him I'm mailing the other half of the bill."

Pug told him and hung up.

"Now you get the idea," I said.

Pug said: "You were trying to muscle in on McGee, weren't you?"

"Maybe."

"Maybe hell, fatty. Why else would he try to run you out of town?"

"All right," I said. "But remember he's going to do the same to you."

"Oh, no, he's not."

"I'll tell you one thing," I said. "McGee has a library with french windows. It's in the back of his house."

Pug scowled at me.

"If anybody should want to . . . see him, he works there every night until one."

Pug gave me a deadpan stare and then went out of the hotel and got in Ginger's car and drove away. I said to the clerk: "If there're any more calls, I'll be back in half an hour."

Chief of Police Piper was drumming on his oak desk with my card. "Sit down," he said. He didn't look up. His round face was tired, and most of the red had gone out of the skin. There were purple veins on his cheeks.

I sat down.

He hit the table with my card again, then stared at it. "We don't like private dicks in Paulton," he said, raising his eyes. He blinked at me. He was thinking he'd seen me before.

"No."

"No." He watched me. "What can I do for you?"

He said it like he wanted to know so he could refuse. I said: "It's more what I can do for you, chief."

"One of those smart ones, eh?"

"I don't know."

"Well, go ahead." He was still curious about my face, but he was tired. "What can you do for me?"

"A couple of things," I said. "How would you like to have another high-class murder in town?"

His mouth came open. "What do you mean?"

"It'd be your bucket, wouldn't it?"

"Now look here . . ."

"You're in a jam," I said. "They're after you because Waterman was killed. Isn't that so?"

His face began to get red.

"And if there's another big killing, you'll be out." I let this sink in, and then said: "And some people will be asking if Pug Banta was really in jail the night of the Papas shooting."

"Pug *was* in jail." The chief made a pretty feeble attempt to roar. "Anybody who says different . . ."

"All right. He was. But some people are saying . . ."

"I can prove it."
"So long as you're chief of police, you can."
He thought this over.
"Somebody's going to try to bump off McGee," I said.
"The lawyer?"
"Either tonight, or some night soon." I told him about the library, and how McGee worked in it late at night. I told him that I'd overheard a couple of men talking about it while I was in the can at Jazzland. I figured I was overworking the gag about hearing things in the can, but I couldn't think of a better story. I said I didn't know who the men were, and that I didn't hear why they wanted to kill him.
"We'll have to warn McGee," the chief said.
"I wouldn't."
"Why?"
"McGee'll give it away. Then you'd never catch the guys. Look, here's the best way. Put a couple of good men in the yard. Then, when they try for McGee, you can grab 'em red-handed."
The idea appealed to him, but he still thought he'd better warn McGee. He hadn't any right to take a chance with him that way, he said. Better to let the killers go than have McGee in danger.
"Wait a minute," I said. "You got a friend named Carmel?"
He nodded before he thought.
"You mean to say," I said, "you *had* a friend."
"Why? What's . . .?"
"Day before yesterday Pug Banta said he wanted to see her, didn't he?"
The chief began to look scared. "You know a hell of a lot, don't you?"
"Pug had you call her," I went on. "Then he met her for you."
I paused. The chief didn't say anything.
"They buried her this morning," I said.
"My God, no!"

I kept letting him have it. "Her body was found outside a town called Valley. She'd been beaten to death."

All the colour had gone out of his face. The veins on his jowls looked green. His eyes were half closed.

I said: "One more thing about McGee."

He looked at me.

"Pug Banta's going to kill him." I got out of the chair. "And if anyone's interested in getting rid of Pug, the place to do it would be McGee's back yard."

He sat at the desk, watched me walk to the door. At the last second he jumped up and trotted after me. He caught my sleeve. "Was she really beaten?"

"Her jaw was shattered, both arms were broken . . ."

"Oh, God! The poor kid!" He tugged my sleeve again. "Say! How do you know this?"

"Her brother called me," I said. "We're old friends. He had to have some dough to bury her."

"Oh, God!" he said.

"Well, so long, chief."

He didn't answer. When I reached the stairs I looked back. He was still standing in the door. I went out of the station into the street. I felt good. Now I had things moving.

CHAPTER 18

NEWSBOYS SELLING an extra in the street outside the hotel woke me up the next morning. I looked at my watch. It was nine o'clock. I telephoned down for breakfast and a bottle of rye.

"Send along one of those extras, too," I told the clerk.

Charles, the Negro, brought the stuff up. I took a shower, drank half a glass of whisky neat and then looked at the extra. Brother, did I get a rear! The headline said: THOMAS McGEE MURDERED. And a subhead said Pug Banta was being held for the job. I sat down on the bed and read the story.

It seemed, the story said, one of Chief Piper's squads had noticed a man lurking around McGee's house. The squad had followed the man (Pug Banta) around to the back, but before they could grab him he shot and killed McGee through one of the french windows in McGee's library. McGee never knew what hit him. The cops then jumped Banta before he had time to move and dragged him off to the station. So far he had refused to say why he'd done the job.

I poured and drank another half glass of whisky. My plan had sort of back-fired, but I didn't know. Maybe it was just as good this way. At least McGee and Pug were out of the road. I lifted the napkin off the breakfast tray and then I got the phone.

"Goddam it," I told the clerk; "I ordered six double lamb chops, not those lousy single ones."

He said he would send up six more right away.

About one o'clock a telegram came. It said:

> Arrive Paulton four pm. Will cut your heart out if you haven't got Penelope.
>
> Grayson.

I had four neat whiskies and a rare steak for lunch, and then I rode out to the Vineyard on the street-car. I sat next to a fat lady with a basket of staples from the A & P, and continued with my thinking. I had a funny feeling that I was close to something, but I was damned if I could tell what it was. I wondered if I had been right about McGee. He had tried to scare me out of town. And he'd known there'd been a robbery at the Vineyard. Yeah, I'd been right. I wondered if he had killed Oke.

"Pardon me."

"Huh?"

"This is where I get off."

"Oh." I let the fat lady and the basket by.

What I'd been hired for, though, was to get Penelope Grayson out. The telegram had reminded me of that. Just thinking about her gave me a sick-empty feeling in my belly. Those damned graves! And that kid Tabitha! And this was the night of the Ceremony of the Bride. I thought again, what a phony idea; the Ceremony of the Bride. But there was nothing phony about those graves. Jesus! I thought, if only there was an honest DA in the county. I wondered what I would say to Grayson. I wondered why I was so worried. I thought at heart I must be a pretty honest bastard.

I went into the Vineyard by the back way. I rolled my knuckles on the door, and the Princess let me in. She looked cool and pretty.

"Honey, did you bring the money?"

"Yes."

"Hand it over."

"I don't know as I ought to."

"Yes, you had, honey. You're in trouble. They got an idea you broke into the vault."

"So McGee told me."

She held out a hand. "Do you want to be caught with the money on you?"

"What about you?"

"They don't suspect me, honey."

I went over and had a drink of the brandy. Then I sat on the divan. "How'd McGee find out?"

"I told him."

"What the hell!"

She sat down beside me and put her hand on my knee. "I had to . . . he knew it anyway."

"How?"

"Well," she said, "one time we discussed breaking into the vault."

"You and McGee?"

She smiled at me. I thought, well, I was right about McGee. I said: "So you worked with him?"

"I still do," she said.

Then I got it. She didn't know he was dead! I wondered why nobody had told her. I decided to stall her.

"Are you in love with him?"

"Oh, no, honey. It's a business arrangement."

"How much does he want?"
"Half. And you got to leave town."
"I'm the fall guy, eh?"
"If the cops come in. But McGee will see they don't."
"How?"
"They're in his pocket, honey. He's the business manager for the Vineyard." She laughed. "You're not such a smart detective."
"I guess not."
"All you have to do is disappear. Later, when everything's quiet, I'll join you. You'll like that, won't you, dear?"
I said "Yes."
"Now where's the money?"
I pulled the roll out of my pants pocket. She counted it. "Where's the other seven thousand?"
"In my wallet."
"Keep it." She put her arms around my neck and kissed me. "Oh, honey, it's not my fault. I love you, honest. McGee's just too smart, that's all."
I tried to kiss her lips, but she wouldn't let me. I wrestled with her for a minute, and then I picked her up and carried her into the bedroom.

Afterwards I lay beside her on the bed. Now I knew everything that had happened. The Elders had told McGee of the robbery and he'd known the Princess was involved because he'd talked over just that kind of a job with her. When he accused her she told him everything, putting me on the spot. Then they made their little plan. I would disappear, and they would blame the robbery on me. *And the murder!* Brother, that was what worried me: the murder! It would be better for them if I never got caught, but nobody would believe my story if I did. They'd have an alibi.
The goddamdest thing was I still couldn't do anything about it, even with McGee gone. The Princess still had the whip. I'd have to take the rap! Or do a bunk. I figured I had about ten grand. That wouldn't last a murder fugitive very long.
"What are you thinking about, honey?"

"About how nice it'll be when we're together."

"We'll have fun."

We'll have fun like hell! I thought. "When do you want me to leave?"

"Right away."

"I can't. Grayson's coming this afternoon. If I'm not around, he'll make a lot of trouble."

She thought about that. "All right, honey. Stay until tonight. And come out here before you go."

"That'll be nice." I scowled at her. "Only I won't like thinking about the Grayson gal."

"Don't think about her then."

"Just tell me one thing," I said. "Who kills her?"

"I don't know."

I touched the soft skin on her shoulder. "You must have heard something."

"All I know is the Elders have a kind of a ceremony in a room next to the one where Solomon lies. That's at midnight. Then they take the Bride into the big room and leave her by the coffin."

"Yeah?"

"And when they come for her in the morning she's dead."

I slid off the bed and got a bottle of brandy and two glasses. We drank.

"Dead how?"

"A knife in the heart. Solomon's knife."

She sat with her eyes half closed, sipping the drink. "It's crazy," she said, "but they believe Solomon comes back and does it. It's his way of keeping in contact with the earth."

"It's spooky," I said. "Do you believe it?"

"A guy that's been dead five years coming back and knocking off someone? Don't make me laugh."

"Well, who does it?"

"You asked me that," she said. "Honey, let's talk about something else." She rubbed my thigh. "You haven't been dead five years, have you?"

I got back to the Arkady just before four. On my way through the lobby the clerk gave me a note. It said:

Me for the peaceful life. Goodbye.
Ginger.

The clerk said she'd checked out at noon. I felt sorry until I remembered she hadn't returned the bracelet. The bitch! I went up to my room, but I hadn't more than poured myself a drink of rye when the phone rang.

"A Mr Grayson to see you."

I went down to the lobby. Grayson was a heavy-set man, almost as big as me, with a large head. He had grey hair. He was wearing a tan Palm Beach suit. We shook hands. "God, what heat!" he said.

"It's been like this all week."

"Where's the girl?"

I said: "Let's go where we can talk, Mr Grayson."

We went into the bar. Grayson had a glass of milk. I had a rye highball. "Well," he said. "Where is she?"

"I'll have her tonight."

"You'd damn well better." He glared at me. "I've paid you ten thousand dollars. You produce or I'll throw you in jail."

"Like hell you will," I said.

That made him angry, but he kept it down. "The hell I won't," he said. "But that's tomorrow. We're friends until then."

"Sure," I said.

"How're you going to get her tonight?"

I told him we were taking the chief of police to the Vineyard in the evening. "We'll crack the place wide open."

"Why haven't you done it before?"

"It's a long story."

"I've got lots of time."

"All right," I said. I told him some of the story, mostly about Oke Johnson, McGee and Banta, but I didn't mention the Princess or the Ceremony of the Bride.

"Then McGee is the man who killed Johnson."

"No," I said.

"Then who?"

"If I'm right it'll be a goddam surprise to a lot of people."

"You'd better tell me," Grayson said.
"Later."
His face got red, but he took it. He was plenty worried about the girl. I wondered how he'd gotten such a red face from drinking milk.
"The chief'll pick you up here at eleven-thirty, Mr Grayson," I said.
His eyes were flat and hard. "You'd better come through."
I got up. "I always come through."
I left him to pay for the drinks. It never does to buy anything for a client.

I went upstairs and called the chief. "I was just going to call you," he said.
"What for?"
"Pug wants to see you."
I told him I'd be right over. I finished the rye and then I went down to the station. The chief was in his office.
"Listen," I said. "Before I see Pug I want to tell you about a job we got to do tonight."
I told him to get a dozen or so men around eleven-thirty and pick up Grayson and go to the Vineyard. There he was to surround the temple and wait for me to tell him what to do.
The chief's face was worried. "I don't know as I ought to fool around the Vineyard. Not without a warrant."
"You'd better," I said; "unless you want me to ask the Governor for some state troopers."
He said, don't get sore. He said, hadn't we played ball before? I said: "Then you'll have Grayson and the men there around midnight?" He said he would.
"Okay," I said. "Now where's Pug Banta?"
The jail smelled of unwashed toilets, and it was damp, like a cellar. A bulb burned in the corridor between the cells, making deep shadows. A cockroach as big as a half-dollar ran on the cement in front of us. I kicked at him and missed.
The chief said in an aggrieved voice: "I don't know why in hell he wants to see you."
The turnkey clanged the metal gate behind us. I said: "Why didn't you bump him off?"

The chief swore so much I could hardly understand him. I gathered his men had double-crossed him. Instead of shooting Pug, they had grabbed him. I wanted to ask him why he hadn't been there, but I didn't. I knew the answer.

"Well, he'll fry," I said.

"I don't know," the chief said mournfully. "I wish he was in some other jail."

We came to a steel door, our shoes making a hollow sound on the cement. A couple of guys in a cell begged for cigarettes. In another cell a woman was weeping. "A drunk," the chief said. The turnkey opened the door and we went into a room with two cells. One of the cells was empty and Pug Banta was in the other.

"If it ain't my fat pal," he said.

They hadn't touched him. I guess he was too important for them to beat up, even with a murder rap hanging over him. I knew the chief would have liked to, because of Carmel. If anybody needed a beating, Pug did.

Pug said: "You guys scram. I want to talk to fatso, my pal."

Chief Piper glanced at me. "Go ahead," I said. "I'll tell you if he says anything you ought to know."

The chief went out with the turnkey. They locked the steel door behind them.

"So you double-crossed me?"

I said: "What else did you expect?"

Pug stood with his hands over his head, holding to the bar. He looked like pictures of a gorilla. There was that same overdevelopment of arms and shoulders and chest. All he needed was more hair.

"I got a couple of things to tell you," he said.

"Go ahead."

"One of 'em is I'm going to get you when I'm sprung." His voice was so deep in his throat I had to move closer to hear him. "I'll get you if it's the last thing I do."

"The only trouble," I said; "is you'll never get sprung."

"Maybe," he said. "Now the other thing . . ." He reached out of the bars with his long arms, caught my coat and jerked me forward. As my face hit the bars he held the coat with his left hand, put his right arm around my neck and then grabbed a bar. He had me in kind of a vice and when he jerked back I thought my neck had broken.

"Now wise guy . . ." Pug snarled. The hand holding the bar kept me from pulling back. I braced with both hands, but it didn't do any good. I couldn't get far enough back to breathe. I felt a terrible pressure behind my eyeballs. I tried to shout, but I couldn't make a sound. My head was bursting. I reached out with my right hand and hit up at Pug's stomach. He couldn't move away without letting go with his right hand. I drove my fist into his groin. He groaned and let go the bar and jerked free.

I got my breath back and said: "Come on and fight, you bastard."

Pug moved in, snarling, and hit me through the bars. I felt my teeth give and tasted salty blood. He tried to hit me again, but I caught his arm and jerked him as hard as I could against the bars. His head hit the steel with a *twack*. I reached both hands through the opening in the bars and clasped them behind his neck. I pulled forward, but the bars were a little too narrow for his head to go through. I pulled, bracing hard with my feet. He tried to claw me, but I kept my legs closed. I gave a big jerk and his head came through the bars, leaving skin behind. One side of his face was a mass of blood. I let go his neck and he tried to pull back, but couldn't. His head was still too big. I stepped closer and punched his face, using both hands. It was like a work-out with a punching-bag. I beat his face to a pulp. At last he slid down on the cement, his head still sticking out the bars. Blood began to pool under one cheek.

I kicked his head a few times; but it wasn't worth while. He was out cold. I wiped the blood from my face with a handkerchief and pounded at the steel door. The turnkey opened it. Chief Piper stared at my face.

"What happened?"

"I bumped my head."

The chief said: "I was afraid Pug might try something."

"He did," I said. "But it didn't work."

CHAPTER 19

I LOOKED at my watch by the arc light over the street-car stop. It was ten minutes past eleven. Fifty minutes and the Ceremony would start. I felt empty. I wanted a drink. I looked to see if I had the flashlight and the pistol I'd taken from the punk. Then I walked slowly down the road to the lane that led into the Vineyard, thinking about what I had to do. Heat lightning flickered in the sky.

The Princess had on black silk lounging pyjamas and Chinese red slippers. The black silk made her skin look very white.

"Hello, honey."

I said "Hello," and got a drink of brandy. I sat on the big divan and drank the brandy. I could feel it grab my stomach. The Princess stood looking down at me. She made me nervous.

"Have a drink, baby," I said. "A farewell toast."

"Did you know McGee had been killed?" she asked.

"Yeah, I read. Too bad."

"Did you know about it this afternoon?"

"No."

Her eyes were a glassy blue. "You didn't frame him, did you?"

"How could I do that?"

"Well, it's damn funny." Her eyes narrowed with thinking. "Both Pug and McGee were after you, and now one's dead and the other's in jail."

"Sure," I said. "I fixed it. They call me Superman."

"God damn it!" she said. "I liked McGee. He had brains."

"Listen," I said. "I didn't frame McGee. And if that's a lie, God strike me dead."

I waited, but nothing happened. Her face got softer looking and she poured herself a drink. Then she came and sat by me on the divan. I could smell her.

"I guess you'll have to take his place," she said.

"Me? You're nuts. I'm leaving tonight."

"You *were* leaving, honey. But now you're business manager of the Vineyard."

"I don't want any part of the Vineyard."

"Don't you?" Her voice was as sweet as if she was talking to a baby. "Suppose the police heard about the robbery? And the murder? And found your fingerprints in the vault?"

"I'd be in a hell of a fix."

"Well, nobody will tell them, honey, as long as you stick around and run things."

"I get it."

"I knew you would." She stared at me, and then she unbuttoned my shirt and ran her hand over my chest. "You're not sore, are you?"

"I don't know."

"A girl likes to have a hold over the man she loves. Can't you understand that, dear?"

"Give me another drink."

She got the bottle of brandy and filled both glasses. I asked: "How long does this last?"

"From now on. Won't that be nice, the two of us together."

"What about your wanting to wear pretty clothes and dance and see shows and go to night clubs?"

"That was just talk, honey. I'm very happy here . . . with you." She leaned towards me. "Honey, you love me, don't you?"

I said: "Sure." I looked at a clock on the table. It said half past eleven. Thirty minutes. The Princess's eyes went to the clock, too.

"Honey, I'm sorry about that girl."

"Not as sorry as I am."

"You couldn't help it."

"I guess not."

She ran her hand under my shirt again. "She wanted to join the Vineyard. She even wanted to be the Bride."

"Yeah," I said; "after she'd been doped a little."

"Don't think about it." She drank her brandy, and then

bit my neck. I tried to kiss her lips, but she wouldn't let me. I still didn't understand it. I saw the clock over her shoulder. Twenty-six minutes to go. She lay with her weight on me. "Darling," she whispered. I ran my hand under the pyjama top. "Yes," she said. "Yes."

Now the clock said ten minutes to twelve. She lay naked on the divan, her breasts soft, the nipples flat, looking like all the whores in the world. Her eyes were closed and her pink lips smiled a little. Her skin was pale against the black satin divan.

I poured a glass of brandy and drank it. Then I filled it again. She opened her eyes and looked at me. "Hello."

"Hello."

"Give me a drink."

I gave her the glass of brandy. She sat up and drank a little. I sat beside her on the divan. She leaned over and kissed my neck. Her lips were wet and cool and soft.

"Honey," she said. "We *are* going to have a nice time."

"Yes."

I kissed her. It was the first time on the lips. It was wonderful. I wondered why she hadn't let me before. I could feel her lips tighten under mine. They were getting warm. It felt like I had kissed an electric battery. I let her go and got up and poured myself another drink. I felt shaky. The clock said eight minutes to twelve.

"You're not going yet?" she asked.

"Pretty soon."

"Not yet, honey." She got off the divan and came over to me. "Not yet." She stood close to me and drank from my glass. She smiled at me. "Karl, do you love me?"

"Yes," I said.

"You don't say that as though you meant it."

"I do."

"Say 'I love you'."

"I love you," I said.

She put her arms around me. The glass fell out of my hand. Her body pressed against mine. Her skin was warm. She kissed my lips. There was that shock again. Her arms around my neck were choking me. I tried to push her away. She held me. I pushed harder.

"That's right," she said.

I got away from her. Her eyes were excited. "Now hit me," she said. "Hit me."

I hit her, really hit her. She went flat on the floor. I bent over her and touched her eyes, but there was no reaction. She was cold. I looked at the clock. Six minutes.

I went into her bedroom and searched for the forty-seven grand. I looked everywhere. I looked in the dresser, in both closets, under the beds, even under the rug. In a chest I found the key to the storeroom and I put it in my pocket. Then I searched the bathroom. In the medicine cabinet, in a paper box of Epsom salts, I found the diamonds. They sparkled in the bathroom light. I put them in my pocket. The Epsom salts gave me an idea. I went through the other medicine. No luck. I jerked the can paper roll. Wound around under the paper were twenty one-thousand dollar bills. That was better than nothing. I wondered if McGee had got the rest.

I went into the living-room. She was still on the floor, but she had come to. She looked at me, her eyes dazed. I got the brandy bottle and tapped her on the head with it. She went out again. I looked to see if there was any blood. There wasn't because of her hair. The clock said two minutes past twelve.

I got a blouse and a skirt from the bedroom and put them on her. Then I dressed myself. I picked her up. She was heavy. I went out the door with her and across the damp grass to the temple. She made a snoring noise breathing. Her hair gleamed in the moonlight. The heat lightning lit up the horizon, but there was no thunder. I carried her in the basement door of the temple. I put her down and lit my flashlight and picked her up again. I carried her past where she had killed the guard to the door to the stairs. I could hear my heart beating, and hers. I carried her up the stairs and put her down. Under the door at the top I could see a dim light. I put out the flashlight and opened the door a crack.

Candles made a smear of light at the end of a long room,

lighting a black cross and the kneeling figures of twelve men. The men were in white and I figured they were the Elders. I smelled incense. A mumble of words came from the men; they were praying. They knelt in a half circle around the cross, their backs towards me. I wondered where Penelope Grayson was.

After a while the men stopped praying and stood up. I got ready to carry the Princess away, but they went single file through a door near the cross. They were loaded down with food and bottles of wine and flowers. A current of air from the open door made the candles flicker, distorted the shadow of the cross on the wall. I heard chanting from the next room, and then I noticed something below the cross. It was a kind of a litter, but with short legs; and on it was a woman. A white cloth covered all her body except her head and her long blonde hair. I walked through the darkness to her. It was Penelope Grayson. Her eyes were wide open, but the pupils were as big as horehound drops. Her face was peaceful. When I put my hand over her eyes she didn't blink. She was full of dope.

They were still chanting in the next room. The voices of the Elders were deep. I tiptoed back and got the Princess. She muttered something and I hit her with the flashlight. I put her down by the litter and jerked off the white cloth. Penelope didn't have such a bad figure. Maybe a little thin, but it had possibilities. There was rouge on her face and breasts. I stripped the Princess and took Penelope off the litter and put the Princess in her place. I pulled some pins out of the Princess's hair so it hung down the way Penelope's had. The chanting stopped, and suddenly I got spooked. I threw the cloth over the Princess and picked up Penelope and the clothes and ran to the stairs. The girl didn't weigh anything at all, and under my palms her skin was cold. She didn't struggle. Maybe she thought it was part of the Ceremony. Outside the door, at the head of the stairs, I put the blouse and skirt on her. They were too big for her. Then I looked in the room.

The Elders were just coming back. They filed in, chanting again, and picked up the litter. They stood under the cross with the litter on their shoulders. Now one of them was singing alone. I caught some of the words:

> She is the choice one of her that bore her.
> The daughters saw her, and called her blessed;
> Yea, the queens and the concubines, and they
> praised her.

I didn't know what the hell that meant. The Elders walked slowly with the litter into the other room. I pulled out my watch and turned the flashlight on it. It was quarter past twelve. Grayson and the chief should be outside by now, but I didn't go after them. Instead I crawled past the cross to the far door and looked through. I saw the big room where McGee and I had looked at Solomon's casket. Four candelabra burned on the gold-leaf altar, and the Elders had set the litter down in front of them. I could see the gleam of the Princess's blonde hair. The Elders were chanting:

> If she be a wall,
> We will build upon her a turret of silver:
> And if she be a door,
> We will enclose her with boards of cedar.

Then an Elder with a clear tenor voice sang:

> I am a wall, and my breasts like the towers thereof:
> Then was I in his eyes as one that found peace.

They turned and walked in pairs down the aisle to the big front door of the temple. The one with the clear tenor voice sang:

> Make haste, my beloved,
> And be thou like to a roe or to a young hart
> Upon the mountains of spices.

Then the last two turned and swung the big door shut. I couldn't hear them any more. I went a little further into the room and got that stink of decaying flesh. It was like the smell of a too-long-dead mule. I stepped to one side of the door, so the candles by the cross wouldn't shine on my back, and waited.

All at once I felt hair rise on the back of my neck. I

couldn't see anything but candles burning in the big candelabra and the light sliding off the Princess's hair, but I was plenty scared. Then I saw it, and I was more scared, even though I knew what was coming. The glass top of the coffin opened and a man sat up. He had on a white robe and above it his face looked blue-white, like fish skin. He got up and stepped out of the coffin. He was very tall; I guess six and a half feet, and very thin. He went to the altar and prayed, kneeling in front of the candles. Wind came through the room, making the candles waver, and he looked around. I crouched in the shadow made by the door. He prayed again and then he took a long knife with a gold hilt off the altar. He went over to the litter, holding the knife against his chest. He pulled off the white cloth and raised the knife high above his head. I could see the golden colour of the Princess's skin by his knees.

I turned and crawled through the door. Behind me I heard a sound, as though somebody had slapped a wall with a wet towel, and then a moan, but, brother, I never once looked back. I got up and ran past the black cross and got Penelope Grayson and carried her down the stairs. She struggled a little; I guess she knew something was wrong. I propped her against the wall in the basement and shuffled through the dark towards the outside door. Suddenly something, almost like a big hand against my chest, stopped me, and I knew then what I had to do before I got the others. I guess I had been going to do it all the time or I wouldn't have taken the key to the storeroom. I unlocked the padlock and lit a match and put the diamonds and the twenty-seven grand of the Vineyard's money back where they had come from. I thought about the rest of the money, but I couldn't do anything about it, and by the time I'd got the padlock closed again I was feeling a little better. I was never cut out for a thief, I guess.

I crossed the basement and went outside. When my eyes got used to the moonlight I saw them. They were waiting by a tree in back of the temple. I recognized Chief Piper and Grayson. About five detectives were there, too.

"We thought you weren't coming," the chief said.

Grayson asked: "Where's Penelope?"
"She's safe."
"Where?" he growled.
I spoke to the chief. "You got the place covered?"
"Yeah. There's a dozen men around."
"Good."
I led them to the temple's basement door. I saw a man standing by the front of the temple; one of the chief's men. We left one of our detectives at the back door.
"Grab anybody that tries to come in," I told him.
"Okay."
We went into the basement. I punched on the flashlight. We went across to the other door. I nudged Grayson. "Here she is," I whispered. I flashed the light on the spot where I'd left her. All I could see was the brick wall and the cement floor. Brother, my heart stood still, as the song says.
Grayson said: "What the hell is this?"
I swung the flashlight around the basement. On the other side I caught a movement. I went that way. She was moving with her face to the brick wall, feeling it with her hand; looking, I guess, for a place to get out.
"Penelope!" Grayson called.
"Shut up," I said.
We went over to her. Grayson took her arm and turned her around. Her eyes didn't look quite so bad. There was a trace of surprise in them. "Where . . . ?" she began.
Grayson said "Penelope, don't you know me?"
We left a detective with her. I led the chief and Grayson and the three other dicks to the inside door and up the stairs. I opened the upper door. The first room looked just as I'd left it, candles still burning in front of the cross.
"Come on," I whispered.
We tiptoed across the room to the door. The Princess was lying on the litter in front of the altar, the white cloth in a pile at her feet. I couldn't see the tall man. We went over to the altar. I heard Grayson's breath rush through his nose. The Princess's left breast was smeared with blood. "That's where Penelope would have been," I told Grayson.
I looked for the gold dagger, but it wasn't on the altar.

The others were staring down at the Princess. "God! What a babe!" one of the detectives whispered. I saw bloody handprints on her thighs.

A deep voice said: "Who desecrates my temple?"

The tall man was coming towards the altar from a corner of the room. He had the dagger in his hand and his eyes were a bright blue, almost as though they were lit up from the inside. He came slowly, his long legs stiff, as though he wasn't used to walking. His face, below the wild eyes, was grim.

"Jesus God!" Chief Piper said. "It's Solomon!"

The man kept on coming. He raised the dagger, holding it in his clenched fist. I saw blood on the blade. Chief Piper screamed, the way a rabbit does when it's being killed, and turned and ran. I felt like running, too. Solomon took two more slow steps and then four of us cut loose at him. The flash of powder blinded me; the reports echoed crazily, hurt my ears. Solomon staggered, as though someone had pushed him, and then, hunched over, ran towards his coffin. We all fired at him, making a noise like a tommy-gun going full blast, but he reached the coffin and fell headlong inside. I guess that was where he wanted to be. We stood with our guns, looking at the coffin.

Chief Piper came back from where he had run to, his face chalk white, his eyes too big for his head. He asked: "Is he dead, boys?"

We walked over to the coffin, keeping the pistols in our hands. Solomon lay on his side. Blood made the robe red in a dozen places, and there was a mess of blood where the lower part of his jaw had been shot away. The gold knife was still in his fist.

I said: "Dead as a mackerel."

The stink was terrible. I looked around the coffin, but I couldn't see where it was coming from. It reminded me again of the Kansas City stockyards.

"What the hell was his idea?" the chief said. "Living in a temple for five years. In a coffin."

One of the detectives began to nose around the altar. I got the white cloth and threw it over the Princess. Grayson went downstairs to Penelope. There was a sound of voices outside the temple, and I went to the door and peeked out. About thirty Elders and Brothers had gathered by the steps, but the chief's men were keeping them back. I suppose they had heard the shooting. The cop by the altar called me, and I went back.

"What is it?"

He put his shoulder against the wall back of the altar and a door swung open. I went in behind him and the chief. Our flashlights showed a small room with a couple of tiny windows near the ceiling. There was a bed, a chair, a bookcase with some books and a dresser. In the dresser the detective found some black robes, sandals, and a rifle with a silencer.

"Remember a guy named Johnson?" I asked the chief.

"The one who was murdered?"

I nodded. "There's the gun that killed him."

We went out into the big room again, the cop carrying the silenced rifle. The chief said: "I think you got some explaining to do."

"Not here," I said. "Bodies always give me goose pimples."

After we'd left Penelope at St Ann's Hospital, we went to an all-night bar. Over a whisky and a steak sandwich I made things as clear as I thought I ought. I told Grayson and the chief I'd found from the records that McGee was the Vineyard's business manager. Pug Banta had killed him, I said, because McGee was trying to get rid of him. I showed them the Legion button I'd found in the temple basement.

"I figured Oke Johnson was killed," I said, "by someone who didn't like him nosing around the temple."

And when I found from Jeliff, the butcher, that he was sending old meat to the Vineyard, I said, I had a pretty good idea Solomon was still alive. "What else would they want decayed meat for but to make a stink?" And if Solomon was alive he'd want to keep it a secret, even if he had to kill Johnson.

"Then old Solomon was still behind everything?" the chief asked.

"Sure."

"How the hell did he get his food?"

"I suppose a couple of Elders fed him. They probably didn't know whether he was really dead or alive."

"He was sure crazy," the chief said.

While Grayson told the chief how he'd happened to hire me and Oke Johnson and then went on to some of the things I'd told him at the Arkady, I ate steak and thought about what I'd done. Usually Justice was supposed to be a tall dame in a white robe, but in Paulton, I decided, if the citizens ever stuck a statue of Justice on the courthouse steps, it would have to be a fat, red-faced guy with a scar on his belly.

That was a laugh, but a funny thing: I'd always played on the Justice team. Even now. Nobody could deny that Banta, the Princess and even McGee had it coming. I felt sorry for Caryle Waterman, but it was his own fault. And I had saved Penelope Grayson. I tried to think how I might have got her out in some other way, but I couldn't. It was a case, as the saying goes, of fighting fire with fire.

Grayson turned to me from the chief and asked: "Would Penelope actually have been the Bride if that poor woman hadn't . . . ?"

I said: "Yeah."

Chief Piper scowled at me. "That brings up the one thing I don't understand."

I drank the rest of my whisky. "What?"

"Why'd the Princess take Miss Grayson's place?"

They both stared at me. "Oh," I said; "she just . . . just wanted to help out."

"Didn't she know Solomon . . . uh . . . and killed the Bride?"

"Neither of us knew that," I said earnestly. "Otherwise she'd never done it." I took a bite of steak. "I'd never have let her. The Princess . . . well, I went for her in a big way."

Grayson said: "You don't seem exactly stricken with grief."

"Well," I said, "being a detective toughens a fellow up, Mr Grayson."

THE LIBRARY OF CRIME CLASSICS®

GEORGE BAXT TITLES

The Affair at Royalties
0-930330-77-3 $4.95
The Alfred Hitchcock Murder Case
0-930330-55-2 $5.95
The Dorothy Parker Murder Case
0-930330-36-6 $4.95
"I!" Said the Demon
0-930330-57-9 $4.95
A Parade of Cockeyed Creatures
0-930330-47-1 $4.95
A Queer Kind of Death
0-930330-46-3 $4.95
Satan Is a Woman
0-930330-65-X $5.95
Swing Low Sweet Harriet
0-930330-56-0 $4.95
The Talullah Bankhead Murder Case
0-930330-89-7 $5.95
Topsy and Evil
0-930330-66-8 $4.95
Who's Next?
0-930330-99-4 $17.95

JOHN DICKSON CARR TITLES

Below Suspicion
0-930330-50-1 $4.95
The Burning Court
0-930330-27-7 $4.95
Death Turns the Tables
0-930330-22-6 $4.95
Hag's Nook
0-930330-28-5 $4.95
He Who Whispers
0-930330-38-2 $4.95
The House at Satan's Elbow
0-930330-61-7 $4.95

The Problem of the Green Capsule
0-930330-51-X $4.95
The Sleeping Sphinx
0-930330-24-2 $4.95
The Three Coffins
0-930330-39-0 $4.95
Till Death Do Us Part
0-930330-21-8 $4.95

WRITING AS CARTER DICKSON
The Gilded Man
0-930330-88-9 $4.95
He Wouldn't Kill Patience
0-930330-86-2 $4.95
The Judas Window
0-930330-62-5 $4.95
Nine—and Death Makes Ten
0-930330-69-2 $4.95
The Peacock Feather Murders
0-930330-68-4 $4.95
The Punch and Judy Murders
0-930330-85-4 $4.95
The Red Widow Murders
0-930330-87-0 $4.95

MARGARET MILLAR TITLES
An Air That Kills
0-930330-23-4 $4.95
Ask for Me Tomorrow
0-930330-15-3 $4.95
Banshee
0-930330-14-5 $4.95
Beast in View
0-930330-07-2 $4.95
Beyond This Point Are Monsters
0-930330-31-5 $4.95
The Cannibal Heart
0-930330-32-3 $4.95
The Fiend
0-930330-10-2 $5.95

Fire Will Freeze
0-930330-59-5 $4.95
How Like An Angel
0-930330-04-8 $4.95
The Iron Gates
0-930330-67-6 $4.95
The Listening Walls
0-930330-52-8 $4.95
The Murder of Miranda
0-930330-95-1 $4.95
Rose's Last Summer
0-930330-26-9 $4.95
Spider Webs
0-930330-76-5 $5.95
A Stranger in My Grave
0-930330-06-4 $4.95
Wall of Eyes
0-930330-42-0 $4.95

BACKLIST

CHARLOTTE ARMSTRONG
A Dram of Poison
0-930330-98-6 $4.95
Mischief
0-930330-72-2 $4.95
The Unsuspected
0-930330-84-6 $4.95
JACQUELINE BABBIN
Bloody Special
0-930330-83-8 $4.95
ANTHONY BOUCHER
Nine Times Nine
0-930330-37-4 $4.95
Rocket to the Morgue
0-930330-82-X $4.95
CARYL BRAHMS & S.J. SIMON
A Bullet in the Ballet
0-930330-12-9 $5.95

Murder a la Stroganoff
0-930330-33-1 $4.95
Six Curtains for Stroganova
0-930330-49-8 $4.95
CHRISTIANNA BRAND
Cat and Mouse
0-930330-18-8 $4.95
MAX BRAND
The Night Flower
0-930330-48-X $4.95
HERBERT BREAN
The Traces of Brillhart
0-930330-81-1 $4.95
Wilders Walk Away
0-930330-73-0 $4.95
LESLIE CHARTERIS
The Last Hero
0-930330-96-X $4.95
The Saint in New York
0-930330-97-8 $4.95
CARROLL JOHN DALY
Murder from the East
0-930330-01-3 $4.95
LILLIAN DE LA TORRE
Dr. Sam: Johnson, Detector
0-930330-08-0 $6.95
The Detections of Dr. Sam: Johnson
0-930330-09-9 $4.95
The Return of Dr. Sam: Johnson, Detector
0-930330-34-X $4.95
The Exploits of Dr. Sam: Johnson, Detector
0-930330-63-3 $5.95
PAUL GALLICO
The Abandoned
0-930330-64-1 $5.95
Too Many Ghosts
0-930330-80-3 $5.95
Thomasina
0-930330-93-5 $5.95

JAMES GOLLIN
Eliza's Galliardo
0-930330-54-4 $4.95
The Philomel Foundation
0-930330-40-4 $4.95
DOUGLAS GREENE with ROBERT ADEY
Death Locked In
0-930330-75-7 $12.95
DASHIELL HAMMETT & ALEX RAYMOND
Secret Agent X-9
0-930330-05-6 $9.95
RICHARD HULL
The Murder of My Aunt
0-930330-02-1 $4.95
E. RICHARD JOHNSON
Mongo's Back in Town
0-930330-90-0 $4.95
Silver Street
0-930330-78-1 $4.95
JONATHAN LATIMER
The Lady in the Morgue
0-930330-79-X $4.95
Solomon's Vineyard
0-930330-91-9 $4.95
VICTORIA LINCOLN
A Private Disgrace
Lizzie Borden by Daylight
0-930330-35-8 $5.95
BARRY MALZBERG
Underlay
0-930330-41-2 $4.95
WILLIAM F. NOLAN
Look Out for Space
0-930330-20-X $4.95
Space for Hire
0-930330-19-6 $4.95
WILLIAM O'FARRELL
Repeat Performance
0-930330-71-4 $4.95

ELLERY QUEEN
Cat of Many Tails
0-930330-94-3 $4.95
Drury Lane's Last Case
0-930330-70-6 $4.95
The Ellery Queen Omnibus
1-55882-001-9 $9.95
The Tragedy of X
0-930330-43-9 $4.95
The Tragedy of Y
0-930330-53-6 $4.95
The Tragedy of Z
0-930330-58-7 $4.95
S.S. RAFFERTY
Cork of the Colonies
0-930330-11-0 $4.95
Die Laughing
0-930330-16-1 $4.95
CLAYTON RAWSON
Death from a Top Hat
0-930330-44-7 $4.95
Footprints on the Ceiling
0-930330-45-5 $4.95
The Headless Lady
0-930330-60-9 $4.95
No Coffin for the Corpse
0-930330-74-9 $4.95
JOHN SHERWOOD
A Shot in the Arm
0-930330-25-0 $4.95
HAKE TALBOT
Rim of the Pit
0-930330-30-7 $4.95
DARWIN L. TEILHET
The Talking Sparrow Murders
0-930330-29-3 $4.95
P.G. WODEHOUSE
Service with a Smile
0-930330-92-7 $4.95